A rattling noise made me jump. It was coming from the hearth. As I stepped back, something fell out of the chimney in a shower of soot and thudded on the tiles.

My first thought was, *a bomb*. Daft I know, but bombs were on everybody's mind at that time. Good job it wasn't, because I just stood gawping at it. When it didn't do anything, I approached and touched it with my toe. Some soot was dislodged and I saw it was a package, wrapped in oilskin and tied with string. I knelt on the rug and picked it up. It was heavy. *Gold sovereigns*, I thought. *Some miser's hoard*. My fingers plucked at the knot. The string loosened. The oilskin fell away.

It was a revolver . . .

ROBERT SWINDELLS

Shrapnel

CORGI

SHRAPNEL
A CORGI BOOK 978 0552 55930 0

Published in Great Britain by Corgi Books,
an imprint of Random House Children's Books
A Random House Group Company

This edition published 2009

1 3 5 7 9 10 8 6 4 2

The Random House Group Limited supports the Forest Stewardship
Council (FSC), the leading international forest certification organization.
All our titles that are printed on Greenpeace-approved FSC-certified
paper carry the FSC logo. Our paper procurement policy can be found at
www.rbooks.co.uk/environment.

Set in 12/16pt Century Old Style by
Falcon Oast Graphic Art Ltd.

Corgi Books are published by Random House Children's Books,
61–63 Uxbridge Road, London W5 5SA

www.**kids**at**randomhouse**.co.uk
www.**rbooks**.co.uk

Addresses for companies within The Random House Group Limited
can be found at: www.randomhouse.co.uk/offices.htm

THE RANDOM HOUSE GROUP Limited Reg. No. 954009

A CIP catalogue record for this book is available from the British
Library.

Printed in the UK by CPI Bookmarque, Croydon, CR0 4TD

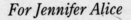

For Jennifer Alice

Spivs

*T*he youth in the natty suit rose, scooping up his companion's empty tankard. 'Same again, is it?'

The other boy frowned, shook his head. 'It's my . . . you got that one. I can't let you . . .'

'Relax, chum. I told you, lolly's not a worry. Back in a sec.'

He watched the suit swerve through knots of young men in uniform, heading for the bar. Must be nice, he thought, enough of the readies to stand a total stranger two rounds in a row, and on a Thursday night. His own wage never stretched past Monday.

'There y'are.' The youth banged two fresh pints on the table. 'Get that down the inside of your neck.' He sat down, sketched a toast with his tankard and took a long pull.

His companion sipped, studying his generous acquaintance over the rim of the glass. 'So,' he said, 'what line are you in, if it's not a rude question?' He smiled in case it was. 'It obviously pays well.'

The youth shrugged. 'I manage.' He grinned. 'Better than slaving in some factory at any rate: beats me how you stick it, mate.'

The boy pulled a face. 'It's a reserved occupation for one thing – I won't be called up.' He sighed. 'Tedious though, day in day out since I was fourteen. I've a good mind to enlist, if only for the chance of a bit of excitement.'

The smart youth shook his head. 'No need for that, chum. If it's excitement you're after, you can find it without getting your head blown off, and have cash in your pocket.'

'How?'

'Easy. Join me. Us. We can always use another bright lad who thrives on excitement.' He smiled. 'Have to leave Mummy and Daddy though, or the Army'll get you.'

The boy smiled. 'That'll be no hardship, I'm cheesed off being treated like a kid. What d'I have to do?'

The youth winked. 'Nothing you'd need a university education for, chum. Drink up.'

ONE

If

'If we had some bacon,' said Dad, 'we could have bacon and eggs, if we had some eggs.'

Mum smiled at this well-worn wartime joke. 'If we had eggs, Frank, we'd be tucking in to one of those rich cakes I used to bake for Sunday tea before the war, instead of this eggless so-called sponge.'

'If I was eighteen instead of thirteen,' I put in, hoovering up dry crumbs with a fingertip, 'I'd be bringing my Spitfire in to land at this very moment, after bagging two Messerschmitts over Kent.'

'If you'd the sense you were born with, Gordon,' snapped Mum, 'you'd thank your lucky stars you're *not* eighteen. Many a lad will have died today, and more'll die tomorrow. I hope it's all over before you're old enough to go.'

'He won't go anyway, Ethel,' said Dad. 'Minute he turns fourteen, he starts with me at Beresford's.'

Hang Beresford's, I thought but didn't say. Beresford's is where Dad works. It's a light engineering factory. In peacetime they make bicycle parts. Now it's shell cases, same as in the Great War. Dad's worked there since he was a boy. He missed the Great War, because engineering was a reserved occupation. It's a reserved occupation this time as well. My brother went there straight from school, but he packed it in a few weeks ago, when he turned twenty-one. You can do what you like when you're twenty-one. He left home at the same time, but he's been seen about so he's not in the Army. Raymond, his name is. I wish he'd taken me with him.

Well, I get picked on, see?

'What colour's Price's dad?' yells Dicky Deadman, and his three chums shout, 'Yellow.'

Their dads served in the Great War. *The last lot*, as it's called now. Deadman senior was in the Navy. Charlie Williams and Bobby Shawcross's dads survived the trenches, and Victor Platt's old man drove an ambulance. Victor's got a sister in the WAAF as well.

Fellows in reserved occupations are doing their bit, but chumps like Deadman don't see it. If you're not in uniform you must be a coward, that's what they reckon.

Proves something I'm about to learn – that war brings out the best in some people, and the worst in others.

TWO

Storm Troopers

Anyway, that was Sunday. Eggless sponge and an evening round the wireless, with boards over the windows so enemy planes won't see our lights.

Monday, back to school. On aerodromes up and down the country, chaps were strapping themselves into Spitfires and Hurricanes, the lucky blighters. No double maths for them. As we shuffled into Foundry Street School, they'd ease back their joysticks and lift clear of the dewy grass, heading for the clouds. While old Whitfield called the register and we said, *'Present, sir'*, wishing we weren't, they'd spot twenty-plus Heinkels and dive on them, machine guns chattering. And by the time we'd copied twelve dreary sums off the board and done them, they'd have landed and be laughing and joking in the mess, while airframe mechanics patched up the bullet holes in their kites. It'd be five years before any of us was old enough to join in, and the fun was bound to be over by then.

'You won't find the answers out there, Price,' snapped Whitfield. I'd been miles away, gazing out of the window.

'No, sir,' I mumbled. 'Sorry. I was just . . .'

'Head in the clouds, laddie. Dreaming. What if our brave soldiers spent *their* time dreaming, eh? Our sailors, our airmen? What d'you think would happen *then*, Price?'

'I . . . dunno, sir.'

'*Don't* you indeed?' He was working himself up into one of his paddies. The kids were smirking behind their hands, enjoying it. Famous for his patriotic rants, was old Whitfield. I reckon he had a conscience about not being in the firing line himself. 'Well, *I* do,' he roared. 'Overrun by Nazi hordes, *that*'s what we'd be. *What* would we be, Price?'

'Sir, overrun by Nazi hordes.'

'Exactly! And what would *you* do about it, laddie?'

'I don't know, sir.'

'Well, *I* do. You'd sit gazing out of the window while storm troopers rampaged through our school shouting *Sieg Heil*, chucking stuff about, ruining our parquet with their jackboots. *What* would you do, laddie?'

I started giggling. Couldn't help it. Well, think about it: husky storm troopers with blue eyes and short blond hair, parachuting into England just so they could make a mess in Foundry Street School. It was ridiculous. But of course he didn't see it.

'Oh, so you think it's *funny*, do you, Price – enemy troops doing exactly as they please in our school? You've a strange sense of humour, so who knows – perhaps you'll find *this* funny as well.' He scrabbled his cane from behind the cupboard, bounded up the aisle between the desks and laid into me with it. I ducked, clasping my hands round my head as he whacked my shoulders and back. It didn't hurt much, padded as I was with blazer, pullover and vest. In fact, as the stick rose and fell I went on giggling, my nose flattened on the desktop. I felt like telling the silly old goat to save his thrashing for the storm troopers, but I didn't.

When he'd worked off his paddy, he said, 'There', like somebody who's knocked the last nail into a really good job, and stalked back to his lectern. I lifted my head. It'd been a hectic minute or so, but it relieved the boredom, and I'd be a sort of hero in the eyes of the class for a while, which would make a nice change.

THREE

Six Thousand Million
Oranges

Most of those who die in air raids are killed by
flying glass. Not a lot of people know that. The
bomb blast blows windows out, and bits of
broken glass whizz through the air. If a little
piece hits you it's like shrapnel – it'll go through
clothes and skin and lodge in your flesh. A big
one'll take your arm off. Or your head. There was
a story in the paper about some poor chap in
London. A bomb went off inside the department
store he was passing and its windows blew out. A
sheet of glass the size of a tea tray hit him, cut
him clean in two. That's why there's an air-raid

shelter in our school yard, and why we have shelter drill once a week.

It's good, shelter drill. Breaks up the day. We had it that Monday morning, right after playtime. It was science, which I quite like, but I enjoy drill even more. We were halfway through watching Miss Robertson make a battery out of copper, zinc and an orange – don't ask me where she found an orange – when we heard the rattle. It's a football rattle. The Head, old Hinkley, stands in the main hall and whirls it, and that's the signal for shelter drill.

What you do is, you drop whatever you're doing and get your gas mask. You put it on, line up and follow your teacher out of the building. The teacher brings the register. You cross the yard and file into the shelter. You do all this calmly, without shouting or shoving. The shelter's a long brick building. It wouldn't stand a direct hit, but it has no windows and no part of it will burn. It's dark inside. Around the walls are narrow benches. You sit with your classmates while your teacher calls the register. That's to make sure everybody's there. Meanwhile old Hinkley and the caretaker check that nobody's in the school before joining us in the shelter.

Sometimes the Head will drone on about something while he's got all of us together. One of his favourites is how you're helping Hitler if you waste food. I quite like this one.

Picture the scene. *Der Fuehrer* in his war room. Huge table covered with maps. He frowns as he studies them. Things aren't going too well. Somebody knocks on the door. '*Komm,*' says old Adolf. It's a fat chap in a fancy uniform. 'Splendid news, *mein Fuehrer* – the young Englander Gordon Price has left two and a half Brussels sprouts on the rim of his plate.' Hitler straightens up, smiling. '*Das ist gut!* Launch the invasion barges – England is ours.'

I'd love to hand that in as an essay, just to see what would happen.

Anyway, this time old Hinkley says, 'Four and a half minutes – well done, everybody,' and we file back to Miss Robertson's battery, which generates enough electricity to make a tiny bulb flicker. I don't see the point. I suppose if we could get hold of about six thousand million oranges we could rig up a fruit-powered searchlight but we can't – there's a war on.

FOUR
DSO

It dragged, that Monday. School days always do of course, even if they're broken up by shelter drill. We finish at four fifteen but it's October, which means it's dusk already. As I made my way along Foundry Street, Dicky Deadman fell in beside me.

'Saw your brother last night,' he said.

'Oh did you?' I couldn't see his three chums, but they'd be nearby. Always were. I kept walking, looking straight ahead. Satchel on one shoulder, gas mask on the other.

'Yes. What does he *do*, Price?'

'Do?'

'Yes. Doing his bit I hope?'

'I . . . dunno actually, Deadman. He's left home, and he's not at Beresford's any more.'

Dicky nodded. 'He wasn't in uniform though. Know what I reckon?'

I sighed. 'What *do* you reckon, Deadman?'

'I reckon he's dodging the call-up. That's why he's left home.'

'Why'd he pack it in at Beresford's then? It's a reserved occupation.'

'Don't ask me, he's not *my* brother. In the family though, isn't it? Dodging, I mean. Your dad dodged the trenches, didn't he? Wasn't wounded like mine, or gassed like Mr Shawcross.'

'Dad's an engineer,' I told him, knowing it was no use. 'The country needs its engineers to keep working in wartime, making stuff the Forces need.'

'That's rubbish, Price, and you know it. Women can do that. And kids. You're a family of shirkers, my dad says. I expect *you'll* go scuttling into Beresford's yourself next year.'

I stopped, faced him. 'If I do, Deadman, it'll be because my dad makes me. I want to fly Spitfires, but you can't at fourteen.' As I spoke I spotted Shawcross, Platt and Williams fifty yards behind, hands in pockets, kicking shoals of fallen leaves at one another. Deadman looked incredulous.

'Fly Spitfires? *You?*' He laughed. 'You couldn't fly a *flag*, you blithering fathead.' He called to the others. 'Hey, you lot, here's the six o'clock news, and this is Dicky Deadman reading it. Price says he wants to fly Spitfires.'

I set off again, but Deadman grabbed my sleeve. 'Not so fast, Squadron Leader. We've got a DSO for you.' He sniggered. 'Not the Distinguished Service Order: the Dodgers and Shirkers Oak leaves. Come on, lads!'

They got me down and shoved handful after handful of dead leaves down my neck. They stuffed 'em in my socks and shoes as well, and filled my satchel. I kicked and struggled, but one man can't fight four. Just before they let me up, Deadman crammed a fistful into my mouth, the dirty pig. They sauntered off chuckling, leaving me curled forward over my knees, choking and retching.

A prince among men, old Dicky.

FIVE

A Shower of Soot

'What on earth have you done to yourself, Gordon?' asked Mum when I got in. My trousers and blazer were crumpled, my shoes were scuffed and there were bits of leaves all over my jumper, but I had my story ready.

'We were playing in the leaves, Mum. Me and some of the chaps. Kicking them around. I'm afraid it got rather out of hand. Sorry.'

Mum tutted, shook her head. 'You're thirteen, Gordon, not three. Go and tidy yourself up, then come and help me with the blackouts. And don't leave a mess in the scullery – you know what your dad's like.'

There was a nasty taste in my mouth and bits of leaf stuck between my teeth. Dust made me itch all over. I could have done with a bath, but that was out of the question. Bath night at our house is Saturday, and today was Monday. A strip-wash at the sink would have to do, once I'd brushed my teeth.

My parents knew nothing about my trouble with Dicky Deadman and his crew. Dad had been roughed up more than once in the Great War for not being in uniform – I didn't feel like telling him the same thing was happening to me twenty-odd years later. And I certainly didn't want him to know that Deadman's dad was calling him a shirker in front of his boy.

I washed, knocked the bits out of my clothes as best I could and put them on again. I raked my scalp with a comb. My mouth tasted minty and I felt better.

Raymond had made our blackouts. Most people use thick curtains for the job, but ours are sheets of plywood. My brother cut them to exactly fit over each window, and screwed little catches to the frames to clamp them in position. It takes two people to put 'em up – one to hold the blackout against the pane, one to turn the catches. Sounds fussy, I know, but if you look from outside you can't see the slightest glimmer of light. No warden'll ever shout at us to *put that light out*, and no enemy pilot will find a target because of us. I should show Deadman our black-outs – tell him Raymond's done his bit.

When Dad got in we had our tea. Mum had made a cheese, tomato and potato loaf. 'Delicious, dear,' said Dad when he'd finished. He's proud of Mum's skill at conjuring tasty dishes out of practically nothing. He looked at her. 'I was thinking we might go to the pictures, Eth. They're showing *The Foreman Went to France* at the Essoldo. Do you good to get away from the kitchen for an hour or two. What d'you say?'

I volunteered to do the washing up, and they went. I like having the place to myself now and then. I found half an hour of dance-band music on the Light Programme. It was Joe Loss and his orchestra – Raymond's favourite. I've missed my brother since he moved out. He's the only person who doesn't treat me like a little kid. When the concert was over I went upstairs to look in his room.

Mum hasn't changed anything. I suppose she hopes he'll move back in one of these days. Bette Davis, Joan Crawford and Dorothy Lamour pouted from the glamour photos he'd cut out of magazines and pinned to the wall. His ukulele stood propped in a corner, and I could see his cricket bat and pads on top of the wardrobe. Even his smell – a mixture of Woodbines and hair-cream – lingered faintly, as though his ghost had just passed through. *There are rooms like this all over England*, I thought. *Young men's bedrooms, empty and waiting. Stuff sitting where it was left – Meccano sets, cigarette cards, tennis racquets, football boots. And each room has its own special smell: that special smell which says Johnnie or Bill or Jack or Albert. And they'll fade and fade, till one day they won't be there any more.*

I don't usually have thoughts like that. Going cuckoo, probably. Anyway, I'd just sniffed Raymond's Bakelite ashtray and put it back on the shelf over the small fireplace, when a rattling noise made me jump. It was coming from the hearth. As I stepped back, something fell out of the chimney in a shower of soot and thudded on the tiles.

My first thought was, *a bomb*. Daft I know, but bombs were on everybody's mind at that time. Good job it wasn't, because I just stood gawping at it. When it didn't do anything, I approached and touched it with my toe. Some soot was dislodged and I saw it was a package, wrapped in oilskin and tied with string. I knelt on the rug and picked it up. It was heavy. *Gold sovereigns*, I thought. *Some miser's hoard.* My fingers plucked at the knot. The string loosened. The oilskin fell away.

It was a revolver.

SIX

Tom Mix and Hopalong Cassidy

You've probably never had hold of a gun. A real one, I mean. They're far heavier than you expect. I blame Tom Mix and Hopalong Cassidy. You see them at the pictures, doing flashy tricks with their Colt 45s, spinning them on one finger and stuff like that. You imagine they weigh about the same as a toy gun, but they don't.

I knelt on the rug, gazing at the weapon in my right hand. It was blue-black except for the grip, which was brown Bakelite. The five-chamber magazine was loaded with dully gleaming, snub-nose bullets. A five-shooter. Never heard of a cowboy with one of those.

I was excited. Breathing fast while my heart hammered at its bony cage. *I've got a gun – a real one. When the invasion comes I can fight.* I grinned. *Keep the storm troopers out of Whitfield's classroom, be the hero of Foundry Street School.*

I knew it wasn't that simple, of course. There's laws about guns, even in wartime. You can't own a revolver unless you've got a licence, and most people don't get licences. That'll be why it was hidden up the chimney.

But whose is it? Can't be Dad's. And nobody else has lived here since before the Great War.

Raymond. This is Raymond's room, so it must be his. But where did he get it from? Why would he want it, and surely he'd have taken it with him when he left?

It was a mystery: the sort boys always hope to stumble across and never do. Well, I'd stumbled across this one, and I wouldn't solve it kneeling on the rug. Mum and Dad'd be home soon. All I could do for now was rewrap the parcel and stick it back up the chimney.

So that's what I did.

SEVEN

Dance

'Good picture, Mum?' It was a quarter past ten, they'd just got in.

'*Very* good thanks, Gordon.' She smiled. 'That Tommy Trinder, I felt like bringing him home.'

'Now then, Ethel,' growled Dad, getting out of his coat. 'Remember you're a married woman.' He looked at me. 'True story, Gordon. This engineer goes across to France to snatch some hush-hush machinery just before Jerry gets his dirty paws on it. Brings it home with help from some Tommies. This was before Dunkirk.' He glances at Mum. 'Trinder's one of the Tommies.'

'He could have Raymond's room,' joked Mum, filling the kettle. I knew it was a joke – my brother's room would stay exactly as it was till he wanted it again.

'Hope there won't be a raid tonight,' I yawned. 'I'm all in.'

'I'm not surprised, young man,' said Mum. 'Look at the time. Drink that cocoa and get yourself off to bed, or you'll never get up for school tomorrow.'

I went to bed, but I couldn't sleep for thinking about the gun in the next room. The more I thought about it, the surer I was that it must belong to my brother. But *why*? What did he want a revolver for? And why would he leave it here?

I knew I ought to tell Mum and Dad about it, but I wouldn't. It'd be telling tales, and no decent chap does that to his brother.

I'll go and see him, I promised myself. *He hasn't gone away. People see him about. I bet he still goes in Farmer Giles. I'll find him and ask. He can only tell me to mind my own business.*

That settled, I treated myself to a fantasy in which I had the gun in my satchel next time the Deadman gang ambushed me. I pulled it out, pointed it at their shoes. 'Dance,' I said, and fired between their feet. They capered about like lunatics, while everybody laughed.

If only life was like that.

EIGHT

So What's New?

It's not a good idea to go home after school and tell your mum you're popping out for a bit. She'll say your tea's nearly ready, or it'll be dark soon, or what if there's a raid. Any excuse to keep you in. Best to do whatever it is you want to do, *then* go home. You might be in trouble for being late, but at least it's mission accomplished.

So instead of turning left on Foundry Street at four fifteen that Tuesday I turned right, heading for the city centre and Farmer Giles. Farmer Giles is a milk bar. In peacetime they serve milk shakes, ice cream and sticky cakes. Now it's weak tea, pretend coffee and a biscuit if you're lucky. It's a place where people meet – local businessmen, wives out shopping, young singles who gather to smoke and chat. My brother's used the place for years.

And there he was, alone at a corner table, smoking. He looked surprised when he saw me. 'What *you* doing down here, kiddo?' He took to calling me kiddo last year. Gets it from American films.

'Looking for you,' I told him.

'Why?' He seemed concerned. 'Mum and Dad all right, I hope?'

I nodded. 'Oh yes, it's nothing like that. Can I sit down?'

He indicated the vacant chair. 'Help yourself. Smoke?'

I grinned, shook my head. He withdrew the packet, regarded me quizzically. 'So, what's new?' *That's* film talk as well.

Now that the moment had arrived, it didn't feel quite so straightforward. For one thing, he'd know I'd been snooping in his room. For another, I'd uncovered something he obviously wanted to keep secret. And lastly, the revolver might not even be his.

'It's . . .' I gulped. *Just say it.* 'There's a gun in your room, Raymond.'

'Ah.' He drew on his cigarette, blew a perfect smoke ring, watched it drift over my head. 'Yes, I know. Do the parents?'

I shook my head. 'No. What's it for, Raymond?'

He shrugged. 'It's for killing people, kiddo.' He sighed. 'Y'know, I thought I'd found a darned good hiding place for it. Do you stick your head up a lot of chimneys, Gordon?'

'I didn't stick my head up. I was there when the gun fell out. It could just as easily have been Mum.'

'What – falling out of the chimney?'

'No, you fathead, I meant . . .'

He laughed. 'I know what you meant. Listen.' His expression grew serious as he leaned across the table. 'In wartime,' he murmured, 'things go on that most people don't know about. You realize that, don't you?'

I looked at him. 'You mean spying, stuff like that?'

He nodded. 'Spying's one thing, but there's a lot more, mostly done by people who aren't in uniform.' He glanced round the room and dropped his voice even lower. 'Why d'you think I packed in my job at Beresford's, Gordon?'

I shook my head. 'I don't know, Raymond. Mum and Dad don't either. They talk about it sometimes.'

He covered my left hand with his right. 'They must never know, kiddo. *Never*. It'd be dangerous for them. It's dangerous for *you*, but you found the gun so I've no option but to tell you the truth.' He gazed into my eyes. 'Can you keep a secret, Gordon? A *state* secret?'

'A *state* secret?'

'Ssssh!' He squeezed my hand. 'Yes. The reason I left Beresfords is, I was recruited to undertake vital work for the Government.'

'Wow!'

'Keep your *voice* down, Gordon, for Pete's sake. What I'm doing – me and a few others – is setting up a secret army to resist the invader if he comes.'

'You mean, besides the *real* army?'

He nodded. 'The secret army will go into action when our forces have surrendered or been wiped out.'

'They *won't* surrender, will they?' I said this

out loud, couldn't help it. 'Mr Churchill said—'

'Ssssh!' He crushed my knuckles. 'They might have to, kiddo. It's not a toy-town army you know, old Adolf's. Look at Belgium, Holland, France. Look at Poland. This isn't a game we're playing.' He looked at me. 'Will you help me, Gordon?'

I gulped. '*Me?*'

He nodded. 'Yes, *you*. There are kids your age in the French Resistance you know – younger in fact. They carry messages. Packages. At night. Their mums and dads don't know. Think you can do that?'

I couldn't believe what I was hearing. None of it felt real. Me, doing secret work for the Government. I'd wake up in a minute.

'Well – are you up to it or not?' asked my brother.

NINE
Eyes Everywhere

'I... I think so, Raymond, yes.'

'Good lad.' He patted the back of my hand. 'Now listen. I want you to go home, act normally. Mum and Dad mustn't suspect anything. Stay away from that revolver – someone'll collect it soon anyway.' He saw my puzzled frown. 'Not while anyone's in, I don't mean that.' He smiled. 'Just do the stuff you always do, all right?'

I nodded.

'And don't go blabbing to your chums. It's tempting, especially when they call you a dodger and stuff leaves down the inside of your shirt.'

'How the *heck* . . . ?'

He grinned. 'Eyes everywhere, kiddo, that's us. There're chaps like your friend Deadman on every street corner – chaps who think they know what's what, when actually they know nothing. People like them're going to need people like us if the worst happens. You won't find 'em kicking leaves about *then* – hiding *under* 'em, more likely, like slugs from the sun.'

When I got in, Mum said, 'You've been a long time, Gordon.'

'Sorry, Mum.'

'Not been playing in the leaves again, I hope.'

'No. I was reading a poem actually, coming along. Rupert Brooke. *The Soldier*. Got it for homework.'

'Ah.' She nodded, rinsing spuds. 'Learned that when *I* was at school. Still remember bits of it: *If I should die, think only this of me* . . . That's the one, isn't it?'

'Yes, Mum.'

'And he *did* die, poor lad.' She smiled sadly, drying her hands on a tea towel. 'Thank goodness you're only thirteen, love. All over before they call on you.'

'Yes, Mum.' I hung my blazer on the newel post and went upstairs, hugging my state secret.

Spivs

'*L*ook, Charlie, it isn't the end of the world. In fact it gave me an idea.'

Charlie brushed an imaginary fleck off his lapel. 'What sort of idea, chum – going to wear the flamin' thing in a fancy holster are you, save the rozzers the trouble of looking for it?' The others laughed.

A train rumbled overhead, shaking the lockup that doubled as HQ and warehouse. The young man waited till train and laughter faded. 'I told him a story,' he continued. 'One he believes because he wants it to be true. He'll do anything I say.

I was thinking about Manley's – the diamonds.'

Charlie shook his head. 'I told you before, mate, we can forget Manley's. Security's tight as a tick's bum – even an inside man's got to leave through the gate and they search 'em. Everyone. You're not going to tell us this kid's the answer, I hope.'

The lad nodded. 'I think he might be, Charlie. Him and a model aeroplane.'

'Model . . . ?' Charlie gazed at the speaker, shook his head. 'You're off your flamin' rocker, chum. Green van'll come for you any minute, padded cell waiting.' Some of the others nodded, chuckling.

The lad shrugged. 'Please yourselves. I could always go solo on this one, keep the dosh myself.'

'Uh – look, Charlie,' put in one man. 'You said yourself the lad's bright. It wouldn't hurt to listen to his idea, surely?'

Charlie sighed, looking down at his immaculate, two-tone shoes. 'All right, chum, let's hear it, and I hope it's a lot better than sticking a shooter up your mum's flamin' chimney.'

TEN
Semolina with Prunes

Mum had just served pudding when the sirens started. It was semolina with prunes, so I didn't care all that much. 'Here we go again,' growled Dad. 'Get the gas masks, Gordon.' We each had a job to do before taking shelter. Mine was to fetch the masks from the coat rack.

Our shelter was at the bottom of the garden. We shared it with the ancient couple next door – the Andersons. The type of shelter we had was called an Anderson Shelter, and the old man had this pathetic joke. 'It's mine, you know,' he'd say,

37

each time we had to take cover. 'Named after me, but it's all right – you can use it, sixpence a time, payable after the war.'

His wife would slap him on the arm and say, 'Ooh, Herbert, you *are* a one,' and we'd all chuckle as if he'd never said it before. As if it was the funniest joke in the world.

The raids themselves were always a disappointment to me. I was mad on aeroplanes, and when we had our first raid I expected to be able to look up and see all the different types: Heinkels, Dorniers, Messerschmitts. I was looking forward to it. In fact you don't see planes at all, just crisscross searchlight beams and blackness. You *hear* 'em, but that just makes it worse. You hear the bombs too, but they don't come screaming down like in films. Flat thuds is what you hear, between the banging of anti-aircraft guns. And you never see a plane get hit – some *do* get shot down, but it's always somewhere else. It's the same as when you watch somebody fishing. You know he's going to hook a fish sooner or later, but no matter how long you hang about watching, he'll never do it while you're there.

'I hope Raymond's taken cover,' murmured Mum as bombs thudded in the distance.

'He'll be right as rain, Mrs Price,' said old Anderson. He'd served in the Boer War, before there were any such things as aeroplanes. 'They can't *see* him, you see.' He shook his head. 'Can't hit a man you can't see.'

'Silly old fool,' muttered his wife. Herbert was a bit deaf and didn't hear.

I smiled to myself in the soily smelling gloom. *He will be right as rain*, I thought. *He has to be, or who'll make sure we have a secret army to challenge the invader?* I didn't half wish I could tell the Andersons, and Mum and Dad, what Raymond and me were doing.

I was thinking this when the world exploded.

ELEVEN

Blast

Blast, they call it. A wall of air moving terrifically fast, outward from the centre of an explosion. Its speed makes it act like something solid – like an express train. It's just a mixture of gases but it blows out windows, shifts brick walls, ruptures eardrums. People have been picked up and hurled through the air by blast.

The bomb landed in the middle of our garden, halfway between the house and the shelter. Its blast ripped the shelter door off its hinges and slammed it against the back wall, buckling the corrugated iron into the packed earth behind it. How that door missed the five of us I'll never know – anybody in its path would have been reduced instantly to pulp.

At the same time, something seemed to suck all the air out of my lungs. For a few seconds I was completely empty, and when I gasped there was nothing to breathe. I was sure I'd die. Then the air filled with dust which I sucked into my throat, starting to choke. I fell down. Somebody nearby was screaming.

'Gordon!' Mum slid her arm under my neck and raised my head. 'Can you hear me – are you all right?'

I nodded. My throat felt clogged. I gipped, puked on her cardigan and croaked, 'Think so, yes. What was it?' The screaming went on.

'A bomb, your dad says. In the garden. He thinks the house is still there.'

'Who's screaming?'

'It's Florrie, love. Mrs Anderson. She's all right – bit of shock, I expect.'

I was breathing more easily. I sat up, screwed up my eyes and shook my head. 'Wow, that was horrible. Can we get out?'

Mum shook her head. 'Raid's still on. Listen for the *all clear*, love.'

Old Florrie stopped screaming and was sobbing in her husband's arms.

Dad turned from looking out and gave Mum a hug. 'That was the one with our name on it, love,' he told her. 'Closest old Adolf'll come to getting us.'

'I hope you're right.' She shivered.

The bangs had stopped. Another few minutes and the siren sounded the *all clear*. Dad climbed the three-rung ladder to ground level, leaned in and helped Mum and the old couple out of the shelter. I came last.

It was dark, but something was on fire a few doors away, and the flickering orange light revealed the state of the garden. Most of it had gone. A great hole yawned between us and the house. The fence which had divided the Andersons' garden from ours lay flattened among ragged remains of lupins and delphiniums. The houses themselves appeared intact, but weren't. Only when we'd edged our way round the crater did we notice there was no glass in any of the windows. None in ours, none in the Andersons'.

'Maybe the fronts'll be all right,' said Dad, but when he and I had picked our way along the side path through a litter of smashed roof tiles, we found that the blast had blown out every pane there too, and the old couple's front door was hanging from a single hinge.

From that night on, I was going to feel completely different about air raids.

TWELVE

Duties to Perform

They took us to a rest centre. They do when you're bombed out. It was a church hall a couple of streets away. Mattresses on the floor, bundles of people's belongings, a few hard chairs. Volunteers showed us where to put our stuff, brought beakers of tea.

Some people spent days and weeks in places like this. The Andersons would. We were lucky. Just the one night, or what was left of it, trying to get to sleep with people mumbling and crying all round, then we were off to my gran's.

Gran was Mum's mum. She lived across town,

on her own. My grandad had died of flu in 1919. 'I'll be glad of the company,' she said.

There were only two proper bedrooms, so I had a camp bed in the attic. It was a Wednesday, but I was allowed to miss school. 'You've hardly slept, love,' said Mum. 'And anyway we'll have to investigate buses, it's too far to walk from here.'

I wasn't grumbling, but I was worried. *What if one of Raymond's people tries to contact me and I'm not there? And then there's the revolver. The blast could easily have knocked it out of the chimney, and there'll be workmen all over the house soon. One of them's bound to notice a package in the hearth, then what?*

'Mum?'

'Yes, love?'

'Would it be all right if I went to the park for a bit? There's a balloon crew there, and I know one of the men.' I played in the park whenever we were at Gran's. A barrage balloon was sited there, and I'd chatted to one of the airmen.

'I suppose so, Gordon, but you mustn't get in the men's way, you know – they have their duties to perform.'

'I know, Mum, I won't be a nuisance.'

'And watch the time – your gran serves lunch at twelve sharp.'

'I'll be here, Mum.'

I don't usually lie to my parents, but I had no choice. I wasn't going to the park. I was off back to our house to check on the gun. Then I had to find my brother, tell him where I was staying. When you're on secret work for the government you have to lie sometimes, and you don't go playing in the park.

The house looked bad in daylight. The roof had lost half its tiles, and some of the window frames had been pushed out. One of Raymond's blackout boards lay cracked in a clump of Michaelmas daisies. And we'd been lucky: the Barkers' house three doors along was nothing but a burned-out shell. Some men were at work there, bracing a dangerous wall with stout timbers.

Nothing was happening at our house, which was good. If the gun had fallen out of the chimney, it should still be on the hearth. I started up the path.

'*Oi!*' One of the workmen was glaring at me across two front gardens. 'Where d'you think *you're* going?'

I stopped, flapped a hand at the house. 'I live here. I need to get something.'

'You need to get right away from there,' he shouted, 'that's all *you* need to get. Don't you *know* it's dangerous to play around bombed houses – don't they teach you *anything* at school? And anyway' – he scowled – 'how do I know you're not one of them *looters*, eh?' Looters were people who went into bombed-out houses and pinched valuables.

I huffed indignantly. 'I'm *not* a looter. I *told* you, this is our house. Everything in it belongs to me and my parents.'

'And what if it falls on you? What then, eh? D'you think it won't squash you flat because it belongs to your dad?'

I glanced at the house. 'Looks all right to me. The walls, I mean.'

He nodded. 'Mebbe it does to you, son, but what do you know? It hasn't been assessed yet, by experts. Blast damage doesn't always show. I'd be on my way if I was you, before I call the rozzers. Or the Home Guard. They shoot looters, y'know, the Home Guard.'

I was bursting to tell him I was doing work for

the Government. Secret work. But if I did it wouldn't be secret, would it? I recalled my brother's words: *chaps who think they know what's what, when actually they know nothing.* He was one, this fellow with his fists on his hips, glaring at me. Calling me a looter. I desperately wanted to tell him I was doing vital work, but I knew where my duty lay. *Walls have ears*, the posters say. *His* wall maybe – the one he and his mates were busy shoring up.

I walked away.

THIRTEEN
Spitfire Parked Outside

Raymond wasn't at Farmer Giles. Nobody was, except the woman behind the counter. It was a quarter past eleven – that dead time between elevenses and lunch. She looked up from spreading margarine on a slice of bread and scraping it off again. 'Looking for someone, dear?'

'Uh . . . no. Not really. I'll try later.' You can't go in a café and tell the waitress you're looking for Raymond Price the government agent, can you? I left, crossed the road, walked up and down.

It was cold. I wished I had the cigarette my brother offered me yesterday, so I could lurk in a doorway like a spy in a film, smoking to look casual. *He might not come,* whispered a voice inside my head. *He doesn't use the place every day.*

To drown out the voice I thought about my classmates. Wednesday morning, last period. Geography with old Contour. His name was Mr Lines but everybody called him Contour. Well, not *everybody.* His wife probably didn't, or the Head. Anyway, he'd be droning on about the North American Grain Belt – picking on someone to point it out on the map, getting ready to bounce the blackboard rubber off the victim's head when he indicated Greenland or Outer Mongolia. *Better the cold street,* I told myself, *than Contour's musty room.*

It was twenty to twelve by the clock over the jeweller's shop when I spotted Raymond. He was walking briskly towards the milk bar with a package under his arm. I made to cross the road, but two lorries came along. By the time they'd lumbered past, my brother was inside Farmer Giles. Through the window I saw him hand the package to the woman. She slipped it under the counter and was drawing a cup of tea from the urn when I walked in.

'Here *again*, kiddo?' queried Raymond. 'What's up – Jerry hit the school last night or something?'

I shook my head. 'No, but he got our house.'

'What?' He stared at me. 'Is everybody all right – Mum and Dad?'

'Yes, we were in the shelter and we've moved in with Gran. I thought I should let you know.'

'You bet!' Hollywood talk again. 'Look here, we'd better sit down for a bit. Tea?'

We sat over steaming cups. I remembered the package. I nodded towards the waitress. 'The lady,' I murmured, 'one of us?'

'Eh?' Raymond frowned, then his brow cleared. 'Oh, yes, one of us, but sssh!'

'Sorry. It was the package. That's how I knew.'

He nodded. 'Good observation, Gordon, well done.' He lifted his cup, looked at me through the steam. 'What's the house like?'

'Oh, it's just the windows. And some tiles. Blast.'

'Could be worse then. Council'll fix that in no time.'

I nodded. 'I've just come from there. Tried to get in, but some workman chased me off. Called me a looter.'

Raymond laughed. 'Some looter. What *did* you want, kiddo?'

I glanced around. The place was filling up. 'You know,' I hissed, 'the whatsit, up the chimney.'

He shook his head. 'You let *me* worry about that Gordon, all right? Don't go back to the house, it might collapse on you.'

'All right. Have you got any work for me yet, Raymond?'

'Not yet. Patience is part of the job, we'll be in touch.'

'At Gran's, remember.'

He smiled, nodded. 'Gran's it is.'

'I've got to go,' I said, 'Gran serves lunch at twelve.'

He looked at his watch and chuckled. 'Never make it, kiddo, unless you've got the Spitfire parked outside.'

I was ten minutes late. I offered to make up the time by not washing my hands, but Mum was having none of it. In fact she made me wash my neck as well.

How many agents does *that* happen to?

FOURTEEN
Sweetheart

'How would you like a bicycle, sweetheart?' *Sweetheart*, for goodness' sake: Gran hasn't noticed I'm not four any more.

I looked at her across the table. 'Wh-what d'you mean, Gran?' I'd been nattering for a bike for at least five years.

Mum broke in. 'I've investigated buses, Gordon, and it's hopeless. Two changes between here and Foundry Street. You'd have to set off at about half-past six every morning. Your gran thinks she can get a bicycle for you. Not a new one, but it'll get you to and from school.'

'Wizard!' I cried. 'Quite a few chaps bike to school. Girls too, of course.' I looked at Gran. 'Where's the bike now, Gran? Whose is it?'

She smiled faintly. 'Well, Gordon, that's the unfortunate part. My neighbours up the road, Mr and Mrs Myers, had a son called Michael. Lovely boy. He joined the Navy, and was drowned last year when his ship was torpedoed. They've put a card in the Post Office window, offering his bicycle for sale. Breaks their hearts to see it in the shed, I suppose, gathering cobwebs.'

After lunch, Gran popped along to see Mrs Myers. She came back wheeling a Raleigh so smart you wouldn't know it was second-hand. I was knocked out. 'It looks brand new, Gran,' I gasped.

She nodded, handing the machine to me. 'Kept all his things nice, Michael Myers.' She looked me in the eye. 'His mum and dad'll see you riding by. They're bound to wish it was Michael in the saddle, but it might be a bit less sad for them if they notice you're caring for his bicycle as he would have done. Will you try to remember that, sweetheart?'

I couldn't speak for the aching lump in my throat. I nodded, blinked watery eyes and wheeled the hero's bike to the shed.

FIFTEEN
Creepy Little Swot

I found myself the centre of attention in the schoolyard Thursday morning. Two reasons, both beginning with b: bombed out, and bike.

'Whee!' shrilled Dicky Deadman as I swept through the gateway. 'What's this, Price – Spitfire practice?' His chums laughed, and the four of them followed me to the bike sheds. I slotted the machine into a stall and fished my gas mask out of the saddlebag. When I turned, the Deadman gang was standing in a semicircle, watching me.

I think there'd have been trouble if old Hinkley hadn't picked that moment to appear.

'C'mon,' muttered Dicky to his chums. 'Time to vanish.' By the time the Head reached me, I was alone.

'Morning, Price.'

'Morning, sir.'

'I understand your family was bombed out on Tuesday night, is that right?'

'Yes, sir.'

'Everybody well though, eh? No casualties?'

'No, sir. We're staying with my gran over Hastley way.' I indicated the bike. 'That's why I've got this.'

'Hmmm, well,' he smiled, 'it's an ill wind, eh? House badly damaged, is it?'

'Not really, sir: glass and tiles mostly. My dad reckons it'll be fixed in a jiffy.'

'That's the spirit. Well – good to see you back amongst us, Price. Let me know if there's anything I can do, won't you?'

There is one thing, sir, I thought but didn't say. *You could give me a year off and buy me flying lessons. Oh, and make Deadman clean the blackboard every afternoon with his tongue.*

As Hinkley walked off, a small crowd gathered. Some sharp-eared tyke had overheard our conversation, and now everybody had questions. How close was the bomb? Did I hear it coming down? Was there a big crater? Had I found its tail, or any good shrapnel? Did I think Jerry was aiming at my dad because he made shell cases?

I'd love to have said no to that last one – told 'em Jerry was after *me* because I was working undercover for the government. I didn't though, of course. If walls have ears, why not bike sheds?

SIXTEEN

OHMS

It wasn't that hard up to now, working with Raymond. In fact I felt a bit of a fraud, thinking of myself as a government agent, or at least *assistant* to a government agent, when all I was doing was keeping quiet about the revolver, and not telling Mum and Dad a state secret. I have to say I liked the feeling of knowing something they didn't though, especially since I was doing it for my country.

But then something happened which took some of the shine off my pleasure.

Breakfast time Saturday, the postman pushed

an envelope through Gran's letter slot. Dad brought it to the table. It was long and brown, with a window. Along the top were the letters OHMS. It was addressed to Mr Raymond Price. Our home address had been scribbled out, and somebody had written *Bombed out – try 6 Trickett Boulevard, Hastley*, which was Gran's address.

'It's for Raymond,' said Mum. 'Looks official. I wonder what it's about?'

'*I* know what it is,' growled Dad. 'It's his call-up papers.'

'But he's in a reserved occupation.'

'He *was*, Ethel,' Dad corrected. 'He chucked his job, now they want him in uniform. I *told* him, but he wouldn't listen.'

'Well – what do we *do* with it, Frank? I mean, I don't want him called up – couldn't we just throw it away, pretend we never got it?'

Dad shook his head. 'Certainly not, Ethel. I'll write *Not at this address* on it, and post it again.'

I stared into my porridge and said nothing. It couldn't be my brother's call-up papers – he was serving already, but I wasn't free to tell them that. I watched Dad write on the envelope. He slid it across to me. 'Pop down to the pillar box with this please, Gordon. When you've finished, I mean.'

I could've taken it to Farmer Giles, left it with the woman if Raymond wasn't there, but what I *really* wanted to do was open it. OHMS stands for On His Majesty's Service. It was probably orders, top secret. I didn't open it – it's an offence to interfere with somebody else's mail and besides, I might be putting Mum and Dad in danger. So I posted it, promising myself I'd mention it to my brother next time I saw him.

Nothing much happened that weekend. Saturday I went to the park, said hello to my balloon crew. There are five of them, all from different parts of Britain, but none from around here. When I mentioned this, Davy from Swansea laughed. 'It's what they do in the Forces, see? They ask where you're from, and post you as far away from home as possible.'

'Aye,' nodded Bristol Pete, 'it's the same with trades. If you was a cook in civvy street they makes you a mechanic, and if you was a mechanic they puts you in the cookhouse.' He winked. 'They found out us five was all scared of balloons when we was kids, so they puts us in charge of a giant one.'

I told them we'd been bombed out, and asked if they'd bring their balloon to fly over our house once it was repaired. It was a joke, of course – they can't choose where to go. 'Our orders are to stay by yer,' grinned Davy. 'Keep Jerry off your gran.'

Sunday morning I biked over to look at our house. I'd polished the Raleigh till it shone, knowing I'd be passing the Myers' place. I'd like to think they saw me pass and approved, but I didn't see anybody and of course you can't stare.

The house hadn't been touched, as far as I could see. It being Sunday there were no workmen about, so I decided I'd risk a quick dekko inside. Dad was borrowing a van and driver from Beresford's in a day or two, to move some of our stuff into storage. I wanted to make sure he wouldn't find my brother's revolver.

It gave me the creeps, going upstairs. *Blast damage doesn't always show*, the man had said last Wednesday, but nothing happened.

There was lots of soot in the hearth – but no package. No gun. To make sure I knelt and felt, and it wasn't there. Somebody'd been here before me.

I went to wash my hands in the scullery, but the water was off. There was no electricity either, or gas. Everything else seemed normal – no sign of looting. I wiped my hands on a floor cloth and left, taking the bike past the Myers' house again.

SEVENTEEN

A *Maid*, for Pete's Sake

Living at Gran's was absolutely wizard. So was sleeping in the attic and biking to school. The only bind was being a long way from the chum I mentioned before, Norman Robinson.

Norman didn't care that my dad hadn't served in the trenches, or that my brother wasn't in uniform. All that mattered to him was that I was as mad on aeroplanes as he was. He was thirteen, same as me, but he didn't go to my school. His dad was a doctor, and Norman attended Woodhouse Grange. *Woodlouse Range*, the Foundry Street kids called it. Your parents had to pay for you to go there. It was probably worth it though – there were no girls, and it had its own rugger pitch and swimming bath.

Woodhouse Grange boys were supposed to be snobs, but Norman wasn't, and neither were his parents: they wouldn't have let him play with *me* if they had been. What we did was buy kits to make balsa aero models. Not the flying ones some chaps made, which never look like the real thing. Ours were perfect little replicas you painted with actual aero dope, then in authentic camouflage and hung on threads from your bedroom ceiling. Mine were in our empty house. Eleven of them: some British, some German. I couldn't rescue them without my parents knowing I'd been inside. I was hoping Dad might collect them when he went with the van.

We usually worked on our models together, Norman and me, in his playroom at the top of their house, which was like a mansion. They even had a *maid*, for Pete's sake.

Anyway, that Sunday afternoon I decided to call at Norman's. I wanted to show him my bike, and tell him where we'd gone. He might not even know we'd been bombed out.

I rode the same route I'd taken that morning. It was a cool, damp day. At the Robinsons' I left my bike at the gate, crunched up the gravel path and rang the bell.

'Oh hello, Gordon.' The maid smiled. 'Norman's been looking for you. Step inside and I'll tell him you're here.'

I nodded. 'Thanks, Sarah.' She hurried away and I gazed around, as I always did. I was standing on a chequered floor of black and white marble, in an entrance hall you could fit our entire house into. There were gilded mirrors, pictures in heavy frames, little antique tables polished to a glow. On one of these stood an ivory telephone. It was like a millionaire's house in a film. You kept expecting George Sanders to appear at the turn of the grand staircase, or Flora Robson. Norman came instead, sliding down the banister with his shirt-tail fluttering. It wasn't the same somehow.

'Gordon, you old rotter – I thought you were *dead*!' He pounded my back, grinning like an idiot. 'I went to your house, it was in ruins. Nobody knew where you'd gone. Did you see the bomber – was it a Dornier?'

I bent under his delighted blows, laughing like a loon. 'Of *course* I didn't see it, you ass, I was in the shelter. We're at my gran's in Hastley. I got a bike.'

'A *bike*?' Norman looked at me. 'Come down with the bomb, did it?'

'No, you moron. My gran bought it from a neighbour so I could get to school. Come and look.'

We capered round each other, throwing dummy punches, kicking up gravel, down to the gate.

'Oh, I say!' He gazed at the sleek machine. 'It's a beauty, Gordon. A Raleigh. Looks new too.' He smiled. 'Lucky you.'

He was being kind, of course. His bike *was* new, the latest model, with a three-speed gear and everything, but Norman wasn't a show-off. It was one of the things I admired about him.

Walking back to the house, he said, 'I got a new kit the other day. Junkers 87. Haven't started it yet.'

I grinned. 'A *Stuka*! I've always wanted a Stuka. They look so . . . evil somehow, with those cranked wings and bow-legs: like iron vultures.'

'I say!' He looked at me. 'Never had you down as a blessed *poet*, Gordon. *Iron vultures*. Mind if I pinch that line, old chap? Go down well at school – might even get it in the mag.'

I shrugged. 'Be my guest.'

'Fair's fair then,' he smiled, 'you can lend a hand with my Stuka. There's a rumour Sarah's liberated a packet of chocolate biscuits from somewhere, needs help disposing of them. Come on.'

EIGHTEEN
Relocated

I sanded down the fuselage while Norman worked on the wings. Kits came with paper plans, showing cross sections of the fuselage at various points. This was so you could shape the thing correctly from the rough block of balsa provided. If you followed the plans carefully you ended up with a model, one seventy-sixth full size, that looked pretty authentic.

'So,' said Norman, squinting along the wing section he was shaping, 'what're you up to when you're not being bombed out, Gordon?'

I shook my head. 'Nothing special, chum.

School, snakes and ladders, prunes and custard.'
I'd love to have told him what my brother was
doing, but of course I couldn't. 'What about you?'

He blew balsa dust off the wing, grinned.
'Three things mostly – homework, homework
and homework. Oh – and there's also homework.' We laughed at our boring lives.

The maid came tapping up the uncarpeted
stairs. She carried in a silver tray with a jug of
home-made lemonade, two glasses and a plate
of chocolate biscuits.

'Thanks, Sarah,' said Norman. 'Where'd you
find the *gorgeous* biscuits?'

The girl smiled. 'Ah, now that'd be telling.'

'*Tell*, then.'

'Telling might mean no more chocolate
biscuits.'

'Why's that?'

'Because' – Sarah rubbed the side of her nose
– 'when somebody finds chocolate biscuits in
wartime, somebody else has probably lost them.'

'You mean they're stolen?'

'Not *stolen*, Norman. Relocated, I suppose you
could say.'

'*Relocated?*' Norman laughed. 'I think you've

been a naughty girl, Sarah.' He offered the plate. 'Here, take one for yourself, and go on being naughty till this bally war is over.'

By tea time the Junkers was assembled, but nude. They're always black in photos; this one looked strange in blond wood – like the *ghost* of a Stuka. We gazed at it.

'Come round tomorrow evening if your people will let you,' said Norman. 'We'll paint it and stick the transfers on.' He grinned. 'With any luck, Sarah might have more goodies squirreled away.' He came out with me and waved as I wobbled off.

'Where have you been, Gordon?' asked Gran when I got in. I'd *three* people quizzing me now, instead of two.

'At Norman's, Gran. We're building a model plane.' I looked at Dad. 'Talking of model planes, Dad, d'you think you could collect mine from the house when you go with the van?'

'Hmmm.' He was filling his pipe. 'Depends.'

'On what?'

'On how much time we have, the condition of the staircase, the state of your room.' He tamped down tobacco with a forefinger. 'Blast might've blown 'em right off the ceiling, y'know – smashed 'em to smithereens.'

'No, they're—' I stopped myself in the nick of time. 'They were pinned quite securely, Dad, I'm sure they'll have survived.'

'Well then.' He struck a match, sucked the flame into the bowl of his pipe. 'We'll see.'

I hate that, don't you? *We'll see.* Leaves you none the wiser.

It was powdered eggs for tea, scrambled, on toast. They come out watery grey, like something the cat brought up. I forced them down though, foiling Hitler's invasion plans once more.

NINETEEN
Two Half-Crowns

After school Monday I cycled into town to see Raymond. Mum didn't know yet how long it ought to take me to get to Gran's, so I needn't watch the time too closely. I'd scrounged two Woodbines and a match from Linton Barker, who claims he's smoked since he was six. I chained the Raleigh to a lamppost across from Farmer Giles and stood in the doorway of a vacant shop, smoking like Humphrey Bogart.

My brother approached the milk bar at twenty to five. I blew out a cloud of smoke, dropped the tab-end, ground it under my shoe and crossed the street with my hands in the pockets of my mac and the collar turned up. It was dusk.

Raymond was at his usual table. Two clippies sat in the window, which was crisscrossed with sticky tape. The same woman was behind the counter. There was nobody else.

'Gordon.' He didn't smile or say sit down.

I sat anyway, leaned across the table. 'A letter came for you.'

'To Gran's?'

'Redirected.'

'Have you got it?'

'No, Dad re-posted it.'

'Not addressed to me *here*, I hope.'

''Course not, he doesn't know you come here. He put, *not at this address*. He reckons it was your call-up papers.'

Raymond nodded. 'Probably was.'

'But . . . ?' I looked at him. 'You're called up already, aren't you?'

'Oh yes, but you see . . .' He glanced across at the clippies, dropped his voice. 'The Secret Service is completely separate from the ordinary Forces, Gordon. The conscription types won't

73

know I've been recruited. The fewer people who know that, the better.'

'So if you don't turn up – for your medical and that – they won't send the police?'

He shook his head. 'Good grief, I hope not, but if they do you mustn't say anything. Don't let on you see me here – or anywhere. In fact, you'd better stop coming here.'

'But I thought . . . how will I know when there's work for me to do?'

He gripped my wrist. 'There *is* work for you to do. Listen carefully.'

My heart kicked me in the ribs and I gulped. 'I'm listening.'

'Good. You still building model planes?'

'Yes – me and Norman.'

'Never mind Norman. He mustn't know anything about the orders I'm going to give you. Understand?'

'Y . . . yes, Raymond.'

'Right. In a minute I'll pass you some money. You're to wait till Saturday, then go to Carter's model shop and buy a Frog Skymaster kit.'

'But . . . ?' I shook my head. 'Frog make *flying* models, we build solids.'

He tightened his grip on my wrist. 'I don't care what *we* do, Gordon. This isn't about *we* – it's about *you*, working solo, undercover and under orders.' He looked me in the eye. 'They don't come from *me*, these orders. I only pass them on. The people they come from expect them to be carried out, and they don't mess around. Let them down and the consequences will be severe. *I* won't be able to protect you. Do you understand?'

I nodded. 'Yes I do, Raymond. Sorry.'

'That's all right then. You will buy a Frog Skymaster. You will take it home and say you bumped into your brother on the street, and he gave you some cash in case he doesn't see you before your birthday. That's how you got the money for the kit. OK so far?'

I nodded.

'Good. You will assemble the model at home, or at Gran's if you're still living there. You will do this very carefully, because your Skymaster must be built exactly according to the instructions provided with the kit.'

'I understand.' *A model plane – what's that got to do with forming a secret army?*

'Righto, here's the cash.' He slid two half-crowns across the table. 'Off you toddle, and don't flash that money around – it isn't ours.'

I looked at him. 'But what do I do with the plane when it's built, Raymond? I don't get it.'

He lit a cigarette, inhaled, talked smoke. 'Follow orders. You'll be contacted. Don't come here again. Goodbye.'

TWENTY
Cabbage Casserole

It was pitch dark as I swerved through Gran's gateway.

'Sorry, Gran,' I said as I walked through the kitchen. 'Long haul from Foundry Street.'

'I know, Gordon, don't worry.' She and Mum were peeling potatoes. You aren't supposed to – it's wasteful, but Gran says potato skins give her the green-apple quickstep. I looked at Mum. 'Is it all right if I go over to Norman's after tea, Mum?'

'Have you no homework, love?'

'Yes, Mum, but it's only science. I'll do it now. We're painting a Stuka.'

'What, in *science*?'

'*No*.' I laughed. 'I mean, me and *Norman* are painting a Stuka.'

'Ah.' Mum nodded. 'So what's your homework?'

'Oh, just a labelled diagram – an orange with zinc and copper rods stuck in it – wires attached to the rods, and a flashlight bulb on the other end.' I grinned. 'The bulb flickers, we did the experiment.'

Gran shook her head. 'Different when *I* was at school. Frogspawn, we did in science.'

'Not in October though, Mum,' said Mum.

The old lady frowned. 'No, it'd be autumn leaves in October, I expect.'

Dad came in at half past five and we had our meal. It was cabbage casserole, which is exactly as exciting as it sounds. Dad made me wipe the dishes for Gran before he'd let me go. 'And think on,' he growled as I fitted my cycle clips, 'eight o'clock and not a minute later. Home Guard shot a lad the other night, mistook him for a saboteur.'

Mum looked at him. 'Where was *that*, Frank? I never heard about that.'

78

'Not far away, Ethel. It wasn't in the paper – bad for morale.'

'You be careful then, love,' said Mum. 'No good being in a reserved occupation and getting shot by your own side.'

I'm not *in* a reserved occupation like Dad, but I didn't say anything – I'd have been there all night. I turned the Raleigh round and set off, pedalling slowly so I wouldn't look like a saboteur, wondering how a Frog Skymaster was going to help England win the war.

'I've got to leave at a quarter to eight,' I told Norman as we climbed the stairs.

'It's after six *now*,' he protested. 'We can't finish the Stuka in an hour and a half.'

'I know. You could let me start, and finish it when I've gone.'

So that's what we did. I doped the 87's underside duck-egg blue while Norman mooched about, adjusting the blackout curtain and choosing where the Stuka would hang among his other planes. Sarah had found no more chocolate biscuits, so all we got was a glass of milk apiece at seven o'clock. The excitement nearly killed us.

I could have livened up the evening no end if I

were free to discuss my other life. *They don't mess around. Let them down and the consequences will be severe. I won't be able to protect you. You will buy a Frog Skymaster. Don't come here again. Goodbye.*

Wouldn't my chum be surprised?

TWENTY-ONE
All Spuds and No Meat

As I lay in bed that night, I realized my new status was more worrying than exciting. There's not much point in having a glamorous job if you can't bask in the glory. And since the whole point of being a secret agent is that nobody must know, there's really no glamour at all. I mean, I don't suppose it's much fun being a fighter pilot really, but at least fighter pilots have wings on their tunics so everybody knows how dashing they are. Being undercover's like being a fighter pilot but wearing a pinstripe suit and carrying a rolled umbrella.

81

Who were they, these chaps who *don't mess around*? And what exactly did that *mean*? What if I let them down by accident, what would they do – shoot me? I'm only thirteen, for goodness' sake.

I never meant to get involved with people who *don't mess around*. Old Whitfield's tough enough for me, and Dicky Deadman. I'm not a hero. Perhaps I ought to tell Raymond I've changed my mind.

Can't though, can I? *Don't come here again. Goodbye.* I'm under orders, and *don't come here again*'s an order, not from Raymond, but from the chaps who don't mess around. I can't go see my brother, so I can't pull out. I'm trapped. A glamorous job that has no glamour's like a wartime meat and potato pie: all spuds and no meat.

I don't know how long it took me to get to sleep that Monday night. I suspect it was Tuesday by the time I drifted off, and then they were in my dream and my brother was right.

They didn't mess around.

TWENTY-TWO
Blithering Nincompoop

Nothing happened on Tuesday. Wednesday we had geography with old Contour. We were doing about wheat. He drew a picture on the board – grain silos in Canada. 'This is where the wheat comes from that goes to make our bread,' he told us. 'Canada grows millions of tons of the stuff every year.' He paused, scanning the five rows of our faces. 'So why is it important that we don't waste bread?' His eyes locked with mine. 'Price?'

'Sir, 'cause there's kids starving in India,' I blurted. It was what Mum always said when I didn't eat up.

Contour snorted. 'Nothing to do with India,' he growled. '*Think*, laddie.'

'Waste not want not, sir?'

'*No*, you blithering nincompoop. *Tell* him, Deadman.'

'Sir, it's the sailors.'

Contour beamed at Dicky. 'What *about* the sailors, Deadman?'

'They're risking their lives, sir, bringing shiploads of wheat through swarms of Nazi U-boats so our mums can put bread on the table.'

'Excellent answer, Deadman.' He looked at me. 'D'you understand *now*, Price?'

'Yes, sir.'

Of *course* I understood, it's exactly what I'd have said myself if he hadn't taken me by surprise. Deadman only knew because his dad was in the Navy in the last war – he probably talks about U-boats all the time.

'Right.' Contour rubbed his hands together. 'You will all copy my picture into your exercise books, label it, and write underneath in your own words what Deadman has just said.' He looked at me. 'Think you can manage that, laddie, or would you like somebody to give you a hand?'

'I can manage, sir, thank you.' *You're a government agent*, I told myself, *surely you can come up with a way to get back at Dicky.*

I don't know what it's like at your school, but mine had kids in it who just *had* to be best at *something*: didn't matter what.

Dicky was best at fighting – he was cock of the school. Somebody else had the hardest conker – a forty-eighter. There was the biggest marble collection, most cigarette cards, highest number of skips without stopping, breath-holding record (Sandra Williams, one minute twenty-two seconds), largest assembly of triangular postage stamps, and so on. But *that* year – 1941 – *shrapnel* was the thing.

Shrapnel is jagged bits of steel. Most of it comes from ack-ack – shells fired by our anti-aircraft guns at enemy bombers. Most of them miss, but they explode in the sky and the fragments rain down all over the place. It's why wardens, firemen and policemen wear tin hats when there's a raid. A piece of shrapnel can kill you if it lands on your head.

And kids collected shrapnel. You could go out the morning after a raid and pick it up off the street. It landed in parks and gardens, and even sometimes in the school yard. Ordinary bits were common – anybody could gather a big collection of those, but certain pieces were rare. The bronze nose cones of shells were real trophies. And bomb tails. One nose cone equalled fifty ordinary fragments, and a bomb tail equalled a hundred. I had a nose cone. Norman had two bomb tails, and if I'd been able to persuade him to give them to me – Woodhouse Grange boys didn't collect shrapnel – mine would have been the second best shrapnel collection at Foundry Street School.

Not the *best*. Walter Linfoot's was easily the best and could never be equalled and I'll tell you why. Walter's big brother was a driver in the RAF. He drove lorries, ambulances and fire tenders. One day he had to drive a Coles Crane to where a German plane had crashed, load it up and take it away. It was a Heinkel 111. He wasn't supposed to, but he snipped a piece out of its tail with bolt cutters and brought it home as a souvenir. It was the centrepiece of Walter's shrapnel collection, pawed and slavered over by every boy in the school.

And it gave me a truly wizard idea.

TWENTY-THREE
Tin Lizzie

It was just after seven when I got to the Robinson residence. Sarah let me in and went off to get Norman. I was gazing at a portrait in a massive gilt frame when he came whizzing down the banister.

'Hullo, Gordon!' he greeted, dismounting. 'Wasn't expecting you tonight.' He nodded at the portrait. 'Colonel Robinson, my grandfather. Made a fortune building cars.'

I nodded. 'I know, you told me. Aluminium bodywork wasn't it – couldn't rust?'

'That's right. Light as a feather, no rust.' He

frowned. 'Beats me why they don't build *all* cars that way.'

'*I* know why,' I said. 'Dad told me. A car like that'd last a lifetime. Nobody'd ever need a new one. Not a good idea if your lolly comes from selling cars.'

Norman grinned. 'Your dad's what they call a cynic, chum.'

I didn't say anything. Couldn't – I don't know what cynic *means*. Chaps who go to Woodhouse Grange pick up all sorts of la-di-da words. I looked at him. 'Funnily enough, your ancestor's car brought me here tonight.'

He pulled a face. 'Not possible, old lad – none on the roads nowadays, worse luck.'

I shook my head. 'I don't mean that. I'm talking about the one your dad's got in his garage.'

'Tin *Lizzie*?' He laughed. 'She doesn't go, you twerp. Hasn't even got an engine. Dad only keeps her because his father built her.'

'Does he look at her much, d'you think?'

Norman shook his head. 'Never, I shouldn't think. She's sat in that murky corner for as long as I can remember. Why d'you ask?'

I winked. 'Tell you upstairs – I want to see what sort of job you made of our Stuka.'

It hung from the ceiling in a near-vertical dive, and he'd done a marvellous job as always. His olive drab met my duck-egg blue in a dead-straight line all the way round, and every transfer was exactly where it belonged. Looking at it, you could almost hear the scream of the sirens on its wheel fairings.

I explained about the colonel's car.

TWENTY-FOUR

Professional Performance

Friday afternoon I was late home on purpose. There was a reason. Tomorrow I'd follow orders and buy the Frog Skymaster at Carter's. Raymond had given me the money last Monday. I'd hidden it inside a wellington boot in the bottom of my wardrobe. This morning I'd smuggled it out in my satchel. Now I had to pretend I'd run into my brother today by accident, and he'd given me the two half-crowns for my birthday, which wasn't until next March. I hadn't been ordered to do any of this, but when you're an agent you're expected to use your initiative when necessary.

'Where've you *been*, Gordon?' asked Mum. 'I *do* wish you'd come straight home from school – especially since Dad told us about the boy who was shot. I worry all the time.'

'Sorry, Mum,' I apologized. 'I bumped into Raymond outside school. He gave me five bob.'

'Five *shillings*?' squeaked Gran. 'What's he doing nowadays – running the Royal Mint?'

'How *is* he, love?' asked Mum. 'Did that envelope reach him?'

I shook my head. 'I don't know, Mum, he didn't mention it.'

'Why did he give you money, Gordon – so *much* money, I mean?'

'For my birthday, in case he doesn't see me again.'

Mum frowned. 'Doesn't *see* you? Why shouldn't he see you – he's not going overseas, is he?'

I shrugged. 'I dunno, Mum, he didn't say, but he's not in uniform.'

'So what does he *do* – where's his money coming from? Shillings don't grow on trees.'

I pulled a face. 'I don't know *any* of his business, Mum. He's found a good job, I suppose. He looks well, I'm sure you needn't worry.'

'Easy for you to say,' she grunted. 'Mothers do worry, can't help it.'

'What will you *do* with your fortune, sweetheart?' asked Gran. 'Save it till March?'

I grinned, shook my head. 'No fear, Gran. There's a wizard flying model in Carter's window – a Frog Skymaster. They're asking exactly five bob for it. I'm off there tomorrow morning, early, before someone else bags it.'

'Someone *else*?' cried Gran. 'There's nobody else in Hastley with five shillings to fritter on toy aeroplanes, young man.'

The Frog Skymaster isn't a *toy* – it's a *model* – but I didn't say anything. Just smiled. I reckoned I'd pulled off my bit of deception really well. Professional performance in fact. Raymond would be proud of me. Him, and the chaps behind him who don't mess around.

I just wished I knew what I was buying the model *for*.

TWENTY-FIVE
Wibbly Wobbly

The box was nearly three feet long. I'd come on the bike. I had a heck of a job getting plane, bike and self home without suffering the most colossal prang. Talk about the wibbly wobbly way.

There was no table in Gran's attic – just a washstand and basin for the maids who'd slept there in the old days. I had to shove my camp bed right into a corner and lay out the plans on the floor. It was bare boards, so pinning down parts while the glue dried would be no problem.

I started straight away. Well, I hadn't a clue

how soon the powers-that-be wanted it finished. *You'll be contacted*, Raymond had said. Didn't say when.

You can't build a flying model in a day. The frame alone consists of more than a hundred strips of balsa. They're held together with glue, which has to dry before you can continue. Everything has to be done in the right order. First the fuselage with the rubber-band engine inside, anchored to the tail at one end and the propeller at the other. Then the undercarriage. Then the wings. The wings are designed to detach for ease of transportation: you can lay them parallel with the fuselage to make a less unwieldy package.

And that's just the frame. After that, the whole thing's got to be covered with tissue-paper, painted with special dope that stretches it taut over the frame and adds toughness, so it won't tear every time the plane hits something, which happens all the time. The dope's transparent, and most modellers add coats of colour for further strength, and to make their models look authentic. I intended doing mine in grey-green camouflage.

I'd only built one wall of the fuselage when Gran called me down for lunch. 'Is it done, love?' she asked.

I shook my head. 'Nowhere near, Gran.'

'Well, you should frame yourself,' she told me. 'They're building *real* ones at the rate of one a day down Avro's.'

'How d'you know?' I asked.

She winked. 'A little bird told me.'

'Little birds should keep their beaks shut,' I rejoined. 'Walls have ears.'

'And boys have hands,' put in Mum. 'Which they ought to wash before eating.'

Aren't grown-ups the giddy limit?

TWENTY-SIX
Better Not To Ask

Every Sunday morning Gran went to church. She went poshed up, with a fur stole and everything. The stole was the pelt of a real fox complete with head, tail and paws. It had glass eyes and a dry, leathery nose. When I was little I liked stroking it, but it made me sad now.

As she looked at herself in the mirror I said, 'Gran?'

'What is it, love?' She was touching up her face with a powder puff.

'Do Germans go to church?'

'I expect so, Gordon. They have lots of pretty churches, I've seen them on postcards.'

'Oh. And will they be asking God to – you know – protect them from bombs, help them win the war?'

She snapped shut her compact, dropped it in her bag, turned from the mirror. 'Bound to, I should think. Why?'

'And it's the same God, isn't it?'

'Ye-es.'

'Well, who will He listen to, Gran? Whose prayers will He answer?'

Gran shook her head. 'I don't know, Gordon. Nobody does.'

'But the Germans'll think He's on *their* side, and we think He's on ours?'

'Something like that.' She looked at me. 'Why not come along – you could ask Reverend Pike your questions, he's more qualified than me.'

'I don't think that's a very good idea, Mum,' put in Dad. She's not *his* mum, she's Mum's, but he calls her 'Mum'.

I looked at him. 'Why not, Dad?'

He shrugged. 'There are some questions it's better not to ask, Gordon – especially in wartime.

And anyway, I thought you were dead keen on finishing that aeroplane of yours.'

I nodded. 'I am. I was just wondering, that's all.' I turned to Gran. 'I won't come, Gran, if that's all right.'

'Of course it's all right, love. I'll see you at twelve o'clock.'

As she turned and left the room, the fox gazed back at me with bright, sightless eyes.

TWENTY-SEVEN
Bad Manners

I finished putting the fuselage together that day. I had the undercarriage in place too, so that the thing stood on the floor like the skeleton of some prehistoric lizard. I wound the rubber-band engine really tightly by turning the propeller. When I let go it spun so fast it pulled the plane across the floor. It only travelled a few feet, but I could tell it'd be absolutely wizard in the air.

The wings would have to be built in the evenings, after homework and between air raids. Attics aren't good places to be during air raids – incendiary bombs come crashing through roofs and set them on fire.

Monday morning I got to school early. So did Walter Linfoot. We had business to see to before the bell.

At morning break there was a crowd round Walter. He had his shrapnel collection out, always an attraction, but that wasn't all. Today he'd decided to cash in on the kids' fascination with his chunk of German bomber by offering to sell bits off it at sixpence a go. Sixpence was a lot of dosh in those days – a week's pocket money for most youngsters – but it's amazing how many of them could get the necessary together if it meant having a bit of Heinkel in their collections. Clearly, old Walter was set to rake in a fortune.

There was a snag however, in the shape of Dicky Deadman, and it wasn't many minutes before he appeared with Charlie, Bobby and Victor in attendance. They shoved their way to the front.

'What's going on, Linfoot?' demanded the cock of the school.

Walter gulped. 'Oh – I've decided to sell bits of my enemy bomber, Deadman – sixpence each. Want one?'

Deadman stared into the lad's eyes. 'Got a

licence, have you, Linfoot? Hawker's licence, to sell on this playground?'

'L . . . licence?' stammered Walter. 'I didn't know I needed a licence.'

'Oooh yes, Linfoot, you need a licence. A hawker's licence. Big trouble if you trade without one.' He grinned evilly. 'Why d'you think spivs make themselves scarce when they spot a rozzer, eh?'

'Well . . . where'll I *get* one, Deadman? Who issues them?'

'Me,' said Deadman. 'On this playground *I* issue 'em, and I'm turning down your application *and* confiscating your stock. Hand it over.'

'No!' Walter clutched the ragged sheet of metal to his chest. 'It's mine. My brother got it for me. You're not having it.'

Deadman turned to his sidekicks. 'Hear that, Bobby, Victor, Charlie? Cheeky runt says I'm not having it. Sheer bad manners, I call that. How about you?'

'Bad manners, definitely,' confirmed Victor.

'Shocking,' nodded Charlie.

'Makes you wonder who brought him up,' growled Bobby. 'Calls for a spot of re-education if you ask me.'

'No.' Deadman shook his head. 'No, he's not a bad lad, old Linfoot. I've known worse.' He looked at Walter. 'I'm feeling generous today, Linfoot, so I'll tell you what I'll do. I'll forget about the licence, and instead of confiscating your stock I'll give you half a crown for it. How's that?'

'Half a *crown*?' Walter looked stricken. 'I'd make half a crown selling five bits, and there must be fifty in this piece. More.'

Deadman nodded. 'That's about right, Linfoot. Fifty at sixpence comes to – what?' Mental arithmetic wasn't Dicky's speciality. Charlie came to his rescue. 'Twenty-five bob I make it, Dicky.'

Deadman nodded. 'Spot on, Charlie, I was just testing.' He thrust a hand into his pocket. 'Here's your half-crown, Linfoot. Take it before I change my mind.'

Poor Walter took the coin and surrendered the precious metal. He even had to lend Deadman the tin-snips he'd brought to cut the pieces with. None of the collectors was sympathetic. They opened a channel to let him through, then clamoured round Deadman offering cash, promises, IOUs. Nothing mattered except their collections.

TWENTY-EIGHT
A Fish in the Sahara

I went nowhere after school that week. Norman probably thought I'd been killed. Straight after tea it was up to my room and on with the Skymaster. Mum was glad, of course. She didn't like me to be out in the blackout, especially since Dad told that story about the boy getting shot. Personally I thought it was nothing but a rumour – there were always unkind stories about the Home Guard. I blame George Formby with that song of his.

Anyway, by bedtime Friday I had the wings built and the whole thing covered, doped and camouflaged. It looked absolutely super and I was dead proud of it. I held it aloft and trotted round the room making engine noises. For a few minutes I forgot I'd built the thing under orders, for a purpose that was a mystery to me.

I had to detach the wings to get the thing down the attic stairs, which were steep and narrow. Mum, Dad and Gran were deeply impressed when I reassembled it on the kitchen table. 'It's splendid, Gordon,' said Mum. 'Isn't it, Frank?'

Dad smiled. 'Yes it is, Ethel.' He looked at me. 'Where will you fly it, son?'

'I ... I'm not sure, Dad.' The question had taken me by surprise. I'd have to wait to be contacted before flying the Skymaster *anywhere*, but I could hardly say that. I shrugged. 'The park, I expect.'

Gran shook her head. 'Not the *park*, sweetheart. Too small. Knock some poor tot's head off with it. Need more space. Myra Shay's big enough, I'd take it there if I were you.' Myra Shay's an expanse of rough grassland halfway between Hastley and school. I biked past it every day.

'Good idea, Mum.' Dad nodded. 'We could try

it out tomorrow afternoon if the rain keeps off.'

We? I went cold. I hadn't a clue about the model's role in my brother's hush-hush work, but I was pretty sure his plans didn't include having Dad around. 'That'll be nice, Dad,' I murmured faintly, 'if the rain keeps off.'

I'm not one for praying, but that night I prayed for rain like a fish in the Sahara.

TWENTY-NINE

Sherlock Holmes Himself

And it rained so hard it woke me up. Two in the morning, drumming on the skylight window of my attic bedroom. I'm not claiming it was my prayer that did it, I'm just saying what happened.

Wet nights were popular that year. Why? Because rain falls out of clouds, and clouds hide everything from enemy bombers. When the moon shone, people spoke of it as a *bomber's moon*. Its light fell on rivers, canals and railway lines, turning them to silver. Bomber crews would follow these gleaming trails to the towns and cities they ran through, and find moon-washed rooftops to aim their bombs at. In 1941, a good wet night was a blessing.

I fell asleep listening to that drumming, and in the morning it was still coming down. I was dead relieved, but I pretended for Dad's benefit to be disappointed. 'Shame,' I murmured, looking out of Gran's parlour window.

Dad nodded ruefully. 'Wouldn't be much fun on Myra Shay this morning, son. Maybe next weekend, eh?'

'Maybe,' I agreed.

I was worried. How would my contact, who-ever he was, know I'd finished the plane? How would he know when to contact me? I thought about it, and an idea came to me. Not much of one, but at any rate the best I could come up with.

What I did was, I stood the Skymaster on the table by the window. It was Gran's best table – polished walnut – so I spread a tea towel over it first. Then I dashed outside to have a squint at it. The plane was clearly visible to anyone walking by. All I could do now was wait.

I didn't have to wait long. Just after ten there was a knock at the side door. Mum opened it, and called to me. 'Young man from Carter's, Gordon, asking for you.'

I hurried to the door, recognized the man who'd sold me the kit. Poor chap looked half-drowned. 'Come inside,' I invited, but he shook his head.

'No time. Manager sent me with this.' He thrust a folded paper at me. 'It's a receipt for five shillings, ought to have given it to you before you left the shop.' He lowered his voice. 'Keep it to yourself, read it, burn it. Good morning.'

He spun on his heel and hurried off, shoulders hunched against the downpour. I stood gawping after him till the penny dropped.

I'd been contacted.

'What did the young man *want*, Gordon?' asked Mum.

I stuffed the paper in my pocket. 'It was nothing, Mum, just a receipt for my five bob. Dunno why they had to send him out on a day like this. I'm off to my room if that's all right.'

Under the skylight I smoothed the paper and

read the words scrawled in pencil:

Fly at Myra Shay Saturday next, ten a.m. Lose plane over Manley's fence, it will be returned in minutes. Do <u>not</u> continue flying, do <u>not</u> examine plane. Leave in shed with bike. Await instructions. Burn this now.

I read the note a second time, then struck a match from the box I kept for the gaslight. The paper was damp, it didn't catch straight away. I held the flame to a corner. My hand shook. I was listening for footfalls but nobody came. Finally the paper caught fire and I dropped it in a Bakelite ashtray, where it burned to a blackened crisp. This I crushed to powder before throwing it out of the window. I rubbed my hands together, satisfied Sherlock Holmes himself couldn't have made sense of it now.

We secret agents can't be too careful.

THIRTY
Bodywork

Another Monday, another double maths session with old Whitfield. I didn't care. There were two good reasons *why* I didn't care. One, I'd been contacted. *Activated*, if you like. I might *look* like the average English schoolboy, bored stiff and longing to get into the war, but I wasn't. I was *in* the war: a secret agent, part of a team of undercover operatives doing hush-hush work vital to the survival of our country. I hadn't a clue what Whitfield's bally x equalled, and I wouldn't be losing any sleep over it.

And two, Dicky Deadman had fallen for a

brilliant bit of spivvery dreamed up by myself, and was about to get his comeuppance.

I closed the trap at morning break. There was a knot of kids round Dicky, who was selling off the last few bits of enemy bomber at the knock-down price of fourpence. Me and Walter Linfoot watched at a distance till they'd all gone, then sidled over. I nodded at the jagged two-inch square he'd kept for his own collection.

'Nice bit of bodywork, that,' I remarked.

He sneered. 'You don't say *bodywork*, Price – not when it's an aeroplane. It's a nice bit of *airframe*, or maybe *fuselage*. Cars have bodywork, you twerp.'

I nodded. 'I know, Dicky, and what you've got there is a nice bit of car bodywork.'

'Don't talk rot, Price. This is off a Heinkel 111. Ask that duffer next to you – *his* brother liberated it.'

Walter shook his head. 'Not *that*, Deadman. The Heinkel's at home. *That*'s a bit off a 1922 Robinson Roadster, and so are all the bits you've flogged at a tanner a time. You're nothing but a cheap fraudster. I wouldn't be you when your customers find out – you'll be a deadman *then* all right.'

Old Dicky. I wish you could've seen his face.

THIRTY-ONE
Not Expecting Jerry

'He's in the conservatory, Gordon, come on through.' I followed Sarah, passing about a million quids worth of antiques and pictures along the way. It'd be a major tragedy if a bomb ever hit this place.

'Gordon!' Norman was sitting in a wicker chair, a stamp album open across his knees. He closed it, set it on a small table and got up. 'I wasn't expecting you.'

I glanced at the powerful lamp on the table, then at the expanse of unshaded glass around and above us. 'You're not expecting *Jerry* either by the look of it – do your parents not *know* about the blackout?'

'Oh, pooh!' He grinned. 'Wardens can't see this side of the house because of the high wall, and it only takes a sec to plunge the place into darkness if the siren goes.' He looked at me. 'Did it *work*, your ruse with the piece we cut from Tin Lizzie?'

I nodded. 'Like a dream. Deadman gave Walter half a crown for it, and made twenty-five bob selling it off in bits. We waited till he sold the last bit, then told him.' I laughed. 'With fifty chaps after his blood, I'm not expecting any more trouble from him in the near future.' I pulled a face. 'I only hope you don't get into hot water with your dad for mutilating the Roadster.'

Norman shook his head. 'I shan't. I told you, he never goes near it and if he did, I'd tell him I donated the piece to the *Saucepans to Spitfires* campaign. He could hardly shout about *that*, could he?'

He was showing me his latest stamp – a cerise Guadeloupe triangular with a beautiful frigate bird on it – when Sarah reappeared. This time there were beakers of rich sweet cocoa and a plate of peppermint-cracknel chocs.

'Y'know, Sarah,' grinned Norman, 'I suspect there isn't a war on at all down your end of the house.'

The girl nodded. 'You're right, Norman – in my quarters it'll always be nineteen thirty-two, and I'll always be seventeen.'

THIRTY-TWO
Just Boys

I could hardly wait for Saturday, when my real work would begin. Something amazing happened on Thursday, but not to me.

Gran knew the people it happened to, they'd been neighbours of hers years ago. Varney was their name. They lived miles away now, out in the country. Mrs Varney had called to see Gran that day and told her the story.

Wednesday night there'd been a raid on the city. An enemy bomber was hit. It turned for home, but one of its engines was on fire and the pilot was forced to make a crash-landing on farmland. Some Home Guard chaps ran to the smoking kite and captured the three-man crew, who were practically unhurt. The nearest house belonged to the Varneys, and the Home Guard knocked them up at two in the morning and asked to use the phone. They had the German airmen at rifle-point. Mrs Varney invited everybody inside, and the prisoners drank tea till the police arrived. They were just boys, Mrs Varney said. Just boys.

'Could they speak English, Gran?' I asked. 'Did they say anything?'

'I don't know,' she told me. 'I didn't ask.'

'Well what about the *plane* – what sort was it? Did it burn up or is it still in the field?'

Gran shrugged. 'I dunno, love, Violet didn't mention it.'

'Were they *armed*, Gran – Lugers or anything?'

'I don't know.'

It was dead frustrating. Why does all the interesting stuff happen during school time? If I'd been there, I'd have asked Violet Varney all sorts. Why couldn't the thing have landed on Trickett Boulevard, and why aren't grown-ups interested in anything except funny wireless programmes such as *ITMA* and when they'll see bananas again?

It was in the local paper a few days later. The story, and a blurry snapshot, just clear enough to make out that the plane was a Dornier, nicknamed the flying pencil. It didn't answer any of my other questions.

I wonder if there's a chap in Germany just like me, building aero models, full of questions only he cares about?

THIRTY-THREE
Sorry

Saturday began dry, but that was all right –
Dad works Saturday mornings, so he couldn't
have come with me to Myra Shay if he'd wanted
to. Whoever was giving me my instructions
probably knew this.

It was hairy, biking with the Skymaster. I'd
detached the wings, of course, and fastened them
with rubber bands to the fuselage, but it still made
an awkward cargo. The bike had no carrier over
the rear wheel, so I had to balance the plane
across the handlebars. Every gust of wind
threatened to topple it and me into the gutter.

I didn't have Myra Shay to myself. There were two dog walkers, and a kite flyer with his mum or older sister. As I assembled the plane, I could see the kite flyer watching. I knew he wanted to come over and look at it, but luckily the girl wouldn't let him. I wound the engine tightly and performed my maiden launch.

It was a wizard first solo. Propeller whirring, the Skymaster soared skyward and went off across the Shay like a golden eagle, while I ran after it laughing like a jackass. For the first time I understood why some chaps prefer flying models to solids. It was as if a part of me was up there, soaring with the plane.

It made a near-perfect landing, bouncing across the turf till it lost speed and a wing tip touched the grass, swinging it round. I picked it up and examined it anxiously. There was no damage.

I looked all around. The dog walkers had disappeared. The young woman was holding the kite-flyer's hand, leading him away. He was resisting, but I could've told him it was no use. A chap about my age had arrived, also by bike, also with a flying model, but he no more wanted to acknowledge me than I did him. There was nobody else. Nobody watching to see how I'd get on, unless they were miles away with binoculars.

I gazed towards the chain-link fence round Manley's. It was nine feet high, with barbed wire coiled along its top. Beyond it ran a cement pathway, and beyond that were some low, red-brick buildings. I wasn't sure what sort of place Manley's was – some sort of storage facility, I thought. Lorries came and went, stuff was loaded and unloaded, but it certainly wasn't a factory. There was no sign of anybody inside the fence. I didn't fancy sending the Skymaster over there. *It will be returned in minutes*, the note had said. By *whom*, for Pete's sake?

Words from a poem came to me:

> *Theirs not to reason why,*
> *Theirs but to do, and die.*

Hoping it wouldn't come to that I rewound the engine, walking towards the fence as I did so. I had to assume the loss of my plane should seem accidental, so I didn't aim at the fence and launch. Instead I waited for a gust of wind, then hurled the machine parallel to the wire. It rose into the wind, banked sharply to port and was carried over, clearing the barbs with a foot to spare. I faked a cry of despair in case someone was within earshot, hooked my fingers through the mesh and watched my pride and joy land heavily on the strip of turf between the pathway and the buildings.

Nobody came so I risked a shout. Well, it's what *anybody* would do who'd lost his plane, isn't it? 'Course it is.

'Hello?' Pause. 'I say, is anybody there?' I rattled the fence. 'Hello?'

There was a wooden lean-to shed. After about five minutes, a fellow emerged from it, muttering to himself. He didn't look at me, but went straight towards the plane.

'Th . . . thanks,' I called. 'Sorry. It won't happen again, I promise.' He ignored me, perhaps he was deaf. He picked up the Skymaster, turned, and went back towards the shed.

'I say, *hello*? It's *my* plane, it was an accident, I'm sorry. D'you think you could . . . ?' He disappeared inside the shed, closing the door.

'It'll be all right,' said a voice behind me. I spun

round. It was the chap I'd seen arrive. He grinned. 'He's scaring you, that's all. Done it to me a couple of times. Makes you think your kite's gone for good, then comes out, swears a bit, chucks it over. You'll see.' He sauntered off, his plane tucked under his arm.

He was right. A minute later the fellow came out with the Skymaster. He glared at me from the path. 'Bleat'n kids,' he growled, 'forever chucking their bleat'n toys over my bleat'n fence. Do it on purpose, I'm bleat'n sick of it.' He lifted the plane high over his head. 'Next time I'll bleat'n stamp on it, see if I don't.' He launched it and it soared over my head.

'Th . . . thanks. I'll fly it over there – *right* over there, you won't be troubled again,' I burbled, but he'd already turned away. I retrieved the Skymaster and trudged towards my bike.

THIRTY-FOUR
Like a Bird

*D*o not *continue flying, do* not *examine plane.*
So I didn't. Had to take the wings off, of
course, but I did it practically without looking.
Strange instruction though, *do* not *examine plane.*
Why not? It looked exactly the same as before,
but still . . .

I fantasized all the way home. *Here's the fear-
less agent, risking life and liberty to carry vital
messages past unsuspecting foes. He will not fail,
the message must get through. He will not crack
under torture: the future of his country is at stake.*

Well, it might be true for all I know.

I stowed bike and plane in Gran's shed and went in to lunch. Dad had just got back.

'Does it fly, son?' he asked as I washed my hands at the sink.

I grinned, nodded. 'Like a bird, Dad – a golden eagle.'

He smiled. 'Splendid. Be sure and tell your brother that, if you ever run across him.'

'Of *course* he'll run across him,' snapped Mum. 'It's not as if Raymond's gone abroad. He's somewhere in the city, not somewhere in North Africa.'

'More's the pity,' growled Dad.

Mum looked at him. 'You don't *mean* that, Frank.'

Dad nodded. 'Certainly I do. At least in Africa he'd be serving his country – lord *knows* what he's up to in the city. No job, money to burn. Upsets me.'

'Well, *I'd* be far more upset if he was away – looking out of the window every verse end, dreading to see a telegram boy coming up the path. I hope he stays in the city till the war's over, no matter *what* he's doing.'

I wanted to tell them. Was dying to say:

Raymond's a secret agent, raising an army to resist the Nazis when they occupy this country. You ought to be proud of him.

But I couldn't, could I?

That night there was a raid, and a tragedy. It was our tragedy as well as other people's, but we didn't find that out for some days.

THIRTY-FIVE
Lucky Girl

The sirens went just after nine. I'd been in bed an hour, but I wasn't asleep. I'd been lying there, thinking about the Skymaster in the shed. What had been the point of today's business at Myra Shay? Was the plane different somehow? A message in invisible ink perhaps, scrawled on a wing by the chap in the lean-to? The siren's wavering howl stopped my wondering.

Dad called from the foot of the attic stairs. 'Shake a leg, son – time to take cover.' I pulled on a jumper over my pyjamas, shoved my feet into slippers and scampered down.

Gran's shelter is just like ours, except she

shares with a mother and baby, not an old couple. The baby was asleep in a clothes basket. At the sound of the first explosion, the mother knelt on the duckboards and bent her body over the basket to shield her baby. I don't suppose it'd have made much difference in the event of a direct hit, but it showed that not all heroes wear uniforms. She stayed like that all night, wouldn't let anybody take over.

It was a very heavy raid, and it went on for hours. Sometimes the ground shook. There were factories in the city where tanks, lorries and aeroplanes were built. The bombers were probably after those, but bombing's never very accurate and we knew lots of houses were being hit as well. I hoped ours wouldn't be among them – repairs had just begun on it.

Our ack-ack was busy, making more racket than the bombs. *Plenty of shrapnel in the morning*, I told myself, *if I'm still here*.

It was nearly dawn when the all clear sounded. The young mother stood up and started knocking dust off her dressing gown. The baby woke and howled.

Gran smiled at it. 'I don't know why *you're*

crying,' she cooed, 'you missed it all, you lucky girl.'

We went in to breakfast. It had to be a cold meal – a main had fractured somewhere, there was no gas. We had water though, which was something.

It was mid-morning when the rumour reached Trickett Boulevard. In the city a railway arch, used as an unofficial shelter, had received a direct hit. More than a hundred people had died, many of them children. None of the dead had yet been identified.

THIRTY-SIX

Knights on a Raft

I'd looked in the shed Sunday morning. The plane was exactly where I'd put it, nothing was different. I was starting to wonder if I was the victim of some complicated practical joke. Was my brother pulling my leg, making me believe I was doing something important when in fact the whole business of the Skymaster and Myra Shay was a wild-goose chase?

I did add some good bits to my shrapnel collection, though I didn't mention it in the house. The grown-ups' mood was sombre because of the railway arch – collecting shrapnel might strike them as callous in the circumstances. After lunch I cycled over to our own house and found it untouched by last night's raid. The roof looked complete. I rode back with the news, which failed to lighten the mood. I felt pretty rotten myself, what with one thing and another.

Tuesday, my world collapsed. *Our* world, I mean. It was tea time. Dad had just got in. We were having knights on a raft – Gran's name for sardines on toast. There was a knock at the door. I jumped up to answer it – I thought it might be the chap from Carter's with fresh orders for me, but it wasn't: it was two policemen with bad news for Dad and Mum. For *all* of us.

They told us Raymond was dead. He'd been one of the people taking shelter under the railway arch. Most of the victims had been stripped of their ration books, identity cards, rings and watches by thieves, before the authorities arrived. This often happened. It made the job of identifying the dead extremely difficult. However, a few bodies had not been robbed, and on one they'd found Raymond's papers.

Mum fell howling to the floor. Gran started

trying to lift her, calling to me to help. Together we got her on her feet and up to her room. When I came down, Dad was shouting at the policemen, saying it must be a terrible mistake – how could anybody be sure who was who in all that carnage?

That was when one of the officers pulled a wristwatch out of his pocket. I'd have recognized it anywhere, and so would Dad.

There'd been no mistake. My brother was dead.

Spivs

'What about taking cover, Natty?' croaked a boy with long, greasy hair.

Natty looked at him. 'Why, got the wind up, have you, Gloria?'

"Course not, Natty, only . . .' He screwed up his eyes as a detonation shook the lockup. 'They're a bit close tonight, I don't fancy—'

'I don't care what you fancy, Gloria. You heard Eric – there's papers galore, everything we need, just lying there. With the Army after half of us and the rozzers one step behind, we need to disappear and this is our chance.' He smirked. 'Just fink, Gloria – you'll be somebody else tomorrer – we all will. Come on.'

THIRTY-SEVEN

Eggless Cake, Watery Smiles

Mum wasn't at breakfast on Wednesday morning. Gran told Dad he ought not to go to Beresford's. He said hundreds of families lost somebody every day – if they all stayed off work, who'd keep the country going?

Then she suggested keeping me off school, but I wanted to go. Till yesterday I'd never seen grown-ups cry, and I didn't think I could face any more of it. Also, I didn't know what to say about Raymond. Now that he was dead, would it be all right to tell Mum and Dad what he'd been doing? I needed them to know he was a hero, but somebody else would take his place and the whole thing was still hush-hush, wasn't it? Keeping my brother's secret was probably the one thing I could do for him now.

We were still doing about wheat with old Contour. Gran had sent a note so the teachers knew I'd lost my brother. In the middle of the lesson, while everybody was drawing a convoy carrying grain across the Atlantic, Mr Lines laid a hand on my shoulder and murmured, 'He was doing his bit, lad, you can be sure about that.' He couldn't know about the secret army, of course, but he'd taught Raymond and must have thought he was a decent lad. Anyway, it was kind.

At lunch time I walked on the playing field by myself. I needed to think. What about *my* work, with the Skymaster? Did it go on, whatever it was, or had Raymond's death ended it? *I suppose*, I told myself, *that if no more instructions come I'll know it's over. Aborted.* I decided all I could do was leave the plane in the shed and wait.

The funeral was on Friday. Dad wouldn't let me go, but I was kept off school so the mourners could see me afterwards at Gran's. She'd opened a tin of ham she'd been hoarding, for sandwiches.

There was tea, and an eggless cake. The parlour was full of relatives, friends and people unknown to me, some in uniform. I was treated to watery smiles and pats on the head.

As soon as I could, I slipped away to the shed. Raymond wasn't *there* either, of course, but his present was. I sat on the floor with the plane in my arms, and cried.

THIRTY-EIGHT

No Guy Fawkes Night

I started feeling sorry for Dicky Deadman. Yes, I know how that sounds, and I can't explain. Maybe when you're hurting, you feel other people's hurt. Anyway, I noticed how he was always by himself, and that he avoided people. Some were after him for their money back, of course. He'd even sold bits of Robinson Roadster to his three chums, and they seemed to have stopped going round with him. Alone, he couldn't sustain his role as cock of the school and he knew it. I suppose what I'm saying is, my plan had worked too well.

November arrived. Usually we'd have great heaps of wood collected by now, ready for Guy Fawkes Night. This year there would *be* no Guy Fawkes Night. There were several reasons for this. One, it's no use having blackout regulations, then lighting up the whole country for Jerry on November 5th. Two, all the fireworks factories had switched to munitions – you couldn't have got a firework for a barrowful of gold. And three, sugar rationing meant nobody's mum would be making bonfire toffee or gingerbread pigs this year. So if you think the war made our lives exciting, you're dead wrong. And if you think it made us all pull together and help one another out, you're wrong again. Every time the sirens sent people hurrying to the shelters, certain other people would creep out under cover of darkness and flit from house to empty house, nicking valuables. They'd even strip the dead, like they did at the railway arch. There *were* good neighbours, of course, but there were these rat-like citizens as well. In fact, it got so bad that people were frightened to leave their properties, and the Home Guard received orders to shoot looters on sight.

No instructions came for me. One day the Skymaster wasn't quite as I'd left it, but the difference was small and it might have been Gran who moved it, or a parent. I didn't dare ask – how would I explain why it mattered? And anyway, the three of them were still raw from grieving, it was wise not to bother them.

Then we got word our house was ready. Gran said she'd miss us, but I reckon she was relieved really.

'D'you think Mr and Mrs Myers'll mind if I keep the bike?' I asked her. I'd be much closer to school, of course.

She said 'It's *yours*, sweetheart, they sold it to us. Look after it, that's all.'

So we went home, and it was there my shadowy controllers got back in touch. *They* didn't call me sweetheart.

THIRTY-NINE

If Wishes Were Horses

I found it in my satchel. It was a Friday evening. I was in my room, getting out my weekend homework. Sandwiched between two exercise books was a sheet of paper. How it got there I don't know – someone must have slipped it in while the satchel was hanging on my hook in the cloakroom. I unfolded it and read this:

Fly Saturday, M.S. Same time, same pilot error. Proceed as before, <u>own</u> shed. Burn this.

M.S. was Myra Shay. *Same pilot error* meant

cross Manley's fence. *Own shed* meant not Gran's. They must think I'm daft – what sort of ass would travel right across town to leave the plane in Gran's shed, just because it said *proceed as before*? I suppose they've got to make absolutely sure.

There's no fireplace in my room, and no matches in Raymond's. I nipped downstairs for a glass of water and pinched a couple of Vestas from the box in the kitchen.

I don't like going in Raymond's room. It looks exactly the same, but he'll never be in it again and that makes it feel different. I laid the sheet of paper in the grate and put a match to it. It burned quickly. I crushed the ashes and left, closing the door behind me.

I'd lost the mood for homework. I lay on the bed and gazed up at my planes. Dad never brought them to Gran's for me after all: said they'd come to no harm where they were, and they hadn't. I didn't half wish I could do a swap – my planes in bits, my brother alive and well.

Gran says *if wishes were horses, beggars would ride*. Means it does no good, wishing. Can't help it though sometimes, can you?

FORTY

Two or Sommink

There was nobody at all on Myra Shay. People have to walk their dogs, even on raw November mornings, but they'd been and gone by the time I got there.

There was no burned patch either. Locals have a huge bonfire on Myra Shay every November. It leaves a big black circle you can see till the spring grass rubs it out. Not this year.

I flew the Skymaster a few times, working my way towards Manley's fence without making it obvious. I no longer wondered whether all this was a practical joke. Who'd keep a joke of my brother's going after his death?

There was no wind today, no excuse for pilot error, but I couldn't help that. I had my orders. If anybody was taking notice they'd know I aimed at the fence on purpose – I just had to hope nobody was.

The plane landed on the cement path, hitting with quite a crack. I stood with my nose to the mesh, wondering what would happen if the Skymaster was damaged – too damaged to fly.

I watched the lean-to door, but that's not where the chap appeared from this time. He came round the end of the main building, stumping along the path with a pick handle in his fist. *A watchman*, I told myself, *on sentry duty*.

He saw the plane, and me, as he was about to go in the lean-to. He changed course and strode towards me, looking furious. I took a step back, though the mesh would've shielded me from the pick handle.

'You again!' he roared. 'You told me you'd play somewhere else, you bleat'n little liar. D'you think I've nothing better to do than fetch your bleat'n toys back, eh? Picking up after you as if you was two or sommink? What if I was to stamp on your bleat'n plane? Feel badly done to then, I suppose. Wait here.' Halfway to the plane, he turned to glare back at me. 'Last time, this. Last bleat'n time, sonny. Do it again and I'll kick it till you can't tell what it is.'

He went and picked up the plane. I half expected him to take it to the lean-to, but he didn't. He stood for a few moments with his back to me, presumably winding the engine, then turned, lifted and launched. The Skymaster came whirring over the fence, apparently undamaged, but when it landed on the lumpy turf the undercarriage collapsed and it did a forward flip onto its back. I ran and picked it up, and when I glanced round the watchman had disappeared.

The undercarriage, which should be springy but firm, flopped about uselessly. Impact with the cement path had torn its wire frame away from the balsa struts inside the fuselage. It would be disastrous to fly the aircraft again before the damage was fixed. It wasn't a big job, but I'd have to strip away some of the doped paper covering the plane's belly. *Do not examine plane.* That was an order, but how was I supposed to repair the thing without examining it?

Back home, I did the only thing I could think of. I left the Skymaster in the shed, unrepaired. I'd leave it till I was ordered to fly again, then fix it before going back to Myra Shay. And if this was the wrong thing to do and they decided to shoot me, what could I do about it?

FORTY-ONE

Cars in Heaven

Sunday morning the plane had been moved, definitely. I'd left it with its propeller facing the door, and now it faced the back wall. And anyway there was a note. Well, hardly a note. One word, scrawled in pencil on the damaged belly:

FIX

Thank you would be nice, I thought. It's one of Gran's sayings. Then I realized whoever wrote it probably meant it to look as though I'd written it myself, in case somebody picked up the plane before I did. We have to think of everything, us agents.

Refixing the undercarriage was a piece of cake, especially now I needn't worry about seeing inside. What made it hard was, Mum and Dad seemed to think that doing everyday things so soon after Raymond's death meant we were forgetting him already.

Dad said, 'Must you do that *now*, Gordon, and your brother not buried a week?'

What was I *supposed* to do? Lie on my bed brooding? Sit in the chair with my head bowed? *Whatever* I did wasn't going to bring him back, was it?

I said, 'Raymond gave me the plane, Dad. He wanted me to fly it. He *still* wants me to. I'm keeping it flying for *him*, like the ground crews do for our fighter pilots.'

Dad was silent for a moment, then he nodded. 'Quite right, son. Keep 'em flying, eh?' He looked across at Mum. 'That's the spirit, isn't it, old girl?'

Mum smiled faintly over her darning. 'Yes, dear, that's the spirit.' She was always close to tears these days.

* * *

146

I was leaving the bike sheds Monday morning when Linton Barker intercepted me. 'Hey, Pricey,' he husked in his twenty cigs a day voice, 'I saw your brother's ghost last night, driving a Morris.' He gave a sticky chuckle. 'Didn't know they dished out cars in Heaven.'

I couldn't speak, but stared at him aghast. He and I have never been enemies – why this appalling joke? I needed to know, but by the time I regained the power of speech he'd thumped my arm and ambled off, bubbling to himself.

FORTY-TWO

Sell his Mother

'How many square feet in a square yard,' snapped Whitfield. 'Deadman?'

'Uh . . . three, sir?' hazarded Dicky, who'd been dreaming.

'Rubbish, that's feet in a yard. *Think*, laddie.'

'I *am*, sir.'

The teacher shook his head. 'No, you're *not*, Deadman. You never do, and I'll tell you why, shall I?'

'Yes please, sir,' said the hapless Dicky. The class tittered.

'You never think, Deadman, because you'll

never *need* to think. You won't bother getting a proper job when you leave us next year. You'll become a spiv instead. Know what a spiv is, do you?'

Dicky nodded. 'A chap wot buys and sells stuff, sir, on the street, out of a suitcase.'

'He's a parasite,' grated Whitfield. 'A black marketeer, stealing goods that belong to the whole nation, selling them at exorbitant prices to the few who can afford them. He's undermining the rationing system, helping the enemy while helping himself to a handsome income without working.' The teacher's voice grew louder as he warmed to his subject. 'The spiv is a *traitor*, Deadman – the lowest of the low. He'd sell his *mother* if he could get half a crown for her. He's selling *England*, laddie – selling everything we're fighting for, just so that he can walk our streets in his sharp suit and ghastly tie, dodging the law, dodging the call-up.'

Whitfield's face was purple now, his hands scrunched into fists. Spit shot through his clenched teeth as he bellowed at poor Dicky. 'And I will not *have*,' he screeched, 'I will not *tolerate*, a fellow of that sort in my classroom. *OUT*, Deadman – *GET OUT.'*

Dicky scrambled to his feet, gazing at that awful face like a bird mesmerized by a snake. He backed towards the door, stammering, 'But, sir, I'm *not* . . . I won't *be* a spiv . . .'

'OUT!' Whitfield groped behind his cupboard, drew out the cane and swished it like a sabre.

Dicky fled.

FORTY-THREE
Job on *ITMA*

'Fag?' Linton Barker held out a Woodbine packet. It was morning break; I'd tracked him down on the playing field.

I shook my head. 'No thanks, you'll get murdered if old Hinkley sees you.' I scowled at him. 'Why'd you say that about my brother, Barker?'

He shrugged. 'Sorry, Price. Chap looked like him, that's all. Didn't mean to upset you.'

'Well, you did. It's no picnic you know, losing somebody.'

He nodded, drawing deeply on his foul

Woodbine. 'I know, my Uncle Peter was on the *Royal Oak*.'

'Really?' The *Royal Oak* was a battleship, sunk in Scapa Flow by a U-boat. Hundreds drowned. 'I never knew that, Barker.'

'No.' He blew out a plume of smoke. 'I don't talk about it. What did your brother *do* anyway, Price?'

I pulled a face. 'I don't know, exactly. *He* didn't talk much either. I think it was important.'

Barker nodded. 'I think we're *all* doing important stuff, Price. You know: carrying on, keeping our end up. Except the spivs, of course. Whitfield was right about them. My dad says they should round 'em all up and shoot them.'

I nodded, then grinned. 'He didn't half lay into old Deadman though, didn't he? Anybody'd think Dicky stood by the gates after school every day, flogging sardines and nylons.'

'Well, he swindled plenty of chaps over those bits of tin he said were from an enemy bomber. Whitfield obviously knows about that.' Linton let out a phlegmy chuckle. 'He ran home, y'know – his mum brought him back just before break. Some cock of the school, eh?'

'Yes,' I murmured, feeling guilty. Dicky's plight was all my fault – I hadn't meant to have him branded a spiv. 'Things aren't exactly ticketyboo for Deadman just now.' I smiled. 'Talking of spivs, did you hear the one about the woman who buys a tin of sardines from a spiv?'

'No.'

'Well, he charges her a shilling for them, and when she opens the tin at home the fish are rotten. So next day she keeps her eyes open and spots the chap on a corner, looking shifty. She marches up to him and says, "You sold me a tin of sardines yesterday, and they were rotten." And he says, "Those sardines weren't for *eating*, darling – they were for buying and selling."'

Barker looked at me. '*Then* what happened?'

I shook my head. 'Nothing. That's it.'

'And that's a *joke*, is it?'

I shrugged. 'It's going round. Sort of a warning, I suppose, against buying stuff off spivs.'

'Yes, well.' He looked at me. 'Don't audition for a job on *ITMA*, will you, Price?'

FORTY-FOUR
Wish I Hadn't

After tea I decided I'd pop across to Norman's. He didn't know about Raymond and I thought it was time he did. You don't keep stuff like that from your best chum. I hadn't even told him we were back home.

'Oh, Gordon,' he said when I broke the news about my brother. 'How utterly awful, your poor parents. How are you managing?'

I pulled a face. 'We're all right, Norman, thanks. Got to be, haven't you?'

He nodded. 'May I tell Dad and Mum? They know about the railway arch – Dad went there next morning – but they've no idea . . .'

'Yes, of course. I'll wait here if that's all right. It's just – I don't like to see grown-ups upset.'

I waited in the playroom under the roof, but I didn't get away with it. A couple of minutes passed, then my chum returned.

'Mum says I'm to bring you down, they want to offer their – you know? I'm sorry.'

It was pretty horrible. They were kind to me, but they were *too* kind, if you understand what I mean. People like the Robinsons, they put everything into *words*. Thoughts and feelings. I mean everybody has them, but most people keep them inside. They're private, and anyway you can't find the right words, they don't come *out* right. Norman's mum managed it, I don't know how. She reminded me of Greer Garson in *Mrs Miniver*. All the time she was talking to me I felt as if we were in a film.

But I know she meant every word.

We went back upstairs, Norman and I, and played with his planes. At half-past eight, just as I was thinking of going home, the sirens went. Naturally the Robinsons made me go with them to their shelter, even though I said my parents would be worried. Doctor Robinson offered to phone them, but we aren't on the telephone. Luckily, it turned out to be a false alarm. No raid developed, and at eleven o'clock the all clear sounded. I was invited to stay the night – Sarah could be sent to tell my people where I was – but I said I had to go.

Something happened as I was biking home which made me wish I hadn't.

There's a short cut you can only take at night. It means crossing a factory yard, and in the daytime its loading bay is always busy – lorries backed up, chaps carrying stuff into them, little trolleys scooting about. It isn't a public right of way, you get shouted at if anybody sees you. There's no night shift though, and because I knew they'd be fretting at home I decided to save a minute.

There was a lorry backed up to the bay. No lights were on, not even the lorry's sidelights. The place was in total darkness. At first I thought the lorry must have been parked there for loading first thing in the morning, but then I saw movement and jammed on the brakes. I was just inside the gateway, practically invisible to a casual glance. I remembered Dad's story of the chap shot by the Home Guard. I stood straddling the bike, absolutely still, hardly daring to breathe.

The loading-bay shutter was up. Men were humping stuff out, passing it over the tailgate to somebody in the back of the lorry. There was no talk. Somebody had a torch, which he switched on briefly now and then. It was a feeble light, but it flitted once across a face I'd know anywhere – a face I'd thought never to see again.

It was the face of my dead brother.

FORTY-FIVE
Zombies

I stood, paralysed with shock. Queer thoughts whirled in my skull. *Ghosts, loading a lorry? Surely not. Zombies, then. In nineteen forty-one, in the middle of England? Don't be an ass. Wish Norman was here. If wishes were horses, beggars would ride, so get a grip, Price, you're a secret agent. Think, laddie.*

Two possibilities. One, it isn't Raymond, just someone who looks like him. After all it was a fleeting glimpse, in feeble light. Or two, it is Raymond and he's alive. The police made a mistake, like Dad said. And the watch? Who knows?

One thing was obvious – whatever was going on here didn't want an audience. The fellows over there on the platform might even be my brother's colleagues – the chaps he warned me about, who *don't mess around*. So instead of standing here like a twerp, waiting to be shot, I'd better make myself scarce.

Moving as stealthily as I possibly could, I started to back away. Each cautious step took me further into shadow, but I never took my eyes off the loading bay. Chaps were still carrying stuff out. The torch flickered now and again, but it didn't find my brother's face. After what seemed like ages, I was out of the yard and free to pedal away.

I was relieved, of course, but my mind was a mess. *Had* I seen my brother? Impossible, surely. A glimpse, a momentary impression. Not *nearly* enough to justify mentioning it to Mum and Dad, upsetting them all over again.

I saw your brother's ghost last night, driving a Morris. Linton Barker's words. Coincidence, nothing more.

Funny though.

A quarter to midnight, I arrived home. They'd

both waited up. My explanation wasn't enough. In fact it wasn't listened to. Dad bawled me out while Mum blubbed. I could have stopped the pair of them dead in their tracks, but I'm not that cruel.

And that's why it couldn't really have been Raymond – he wasn't that cruel either.

FORTY-SIX
Blue Funk

Next day I couldn't concentrate on anything. I was yelled at in history and caned, one on each hand, in Divinity. There seemed to be a little cinematograph inside my head. It kept projecting the same fragment of film – a face, seen fleetingly in the beam from a flashlight. And each time, the face came to look more and more like Raymond's.

It was a talkie too. *Is your brother alive?* it asked, over and over. *Is your brother alive?* It was driving me batty.

I *must* have been batty, because I didn't go

home at home time. I biked into town, chained the Raleigh to the lamp post and stood in the doorway of the vacant shop, just like before. Two things were different – I'd scrounged no fags from Linton Barker, and I was waiting for a dead man.

And he didn't come. Of course he didn't. I waited till the jeweller's clock said five, then crossed to Farmer Giles. Inside I went straight to the counter where the same woman stood.

'Hello,' I said. She looked at me as if she'd never seen me before. 'I wonder if you can help me?'

'*Help* you, dearie?' she said. 'Why, is something the matter?'

'I . . . I'm looking for my brother, he comes in here a lot. You know – Raymond?'

The woman looked baffled, shook her head. 'I don't know any gentleman of that name,' she told me. 'Sorry.'

'Yes you do, I've sat with him, over there.'

She shrugged. 'I serve a lot of people, dearie. Hundreds, I shouldn't wonder. Don't learn most of their faces, and as for *names* . . .'

'Yes, but Raymond's one of *you*.' I whispered

this, glancing around. There were five men at two tables, busy chatting. 'You *know*?'

'One of *me*? I'm sure I don't know what you're talking about, young man.'

'Oh, look.' I leaned in. 'I *know* it's all hush-hush, but that's all right – *I'*m one of you as well.'

She was becoming angry. 'You're one of them *crackpots* if you ask me – one of them *loonies*. It's blast, I expect. I want you to leave now, or I'll call on one of these gentlemen here to show you the door.'

I walked out. The cold air must have brought me to my senses, because as I unchained the bike I thought: *What have I done? Why did I come here, mentioning Raymond's name? What about the chaps who don't mess around? She'll tell 'em. Bound to. Young Price is cracking up.*

I rode home in a blue funk. They'd shoot me for blabbing. I'm probably pedalling into the telescopic sight of someone's high-powered rifle at this moment.

BANG!

Home Guard, they'll say, *mistook the poor kid for a saboteur.*

Easy as that.

FORTY-SEVEN
Ruminating

I hardly slept, got up Wednesday morning with red eyes and raw nerves. It was porridge again. I growled 'not porridge again,' and pushed my bowl away. 'There's a war on, son,' said Dad in a dangerously mild tone, and Mum said, 'What on earth's the matter with you, Gordon – anybody'd think you'd spent the night in the shelter.'

I couldn't *tell* them, could I? Couldn't say, *I'm scared. I've got myself into something dangerous and now I could die, just because I wanted a bit of glamour, bit of excitement.* I wanted to – *longed* to – but I was trapped, like the lad who volunteers as a fighter pilot so he'll have wings on his tunic and girls all over him, then finds the likely prospect of being fried to a crisp in a burning plane completely swamps any glamour there might be in it.

Truth is, I was getting cheesed off not being able to talk to anybody about the important things in my life. I mean, what's the use of parents, chums and teachers if you can't confide in them?

The life of the secret agent is a lonely one. And if you think that's got a romantic ring to it, try it.

Last period Wednesday morning is geography. We've finished wheat, the class is doing corned beef. The *class* is, I'm not. I'm ruminating. Ruminating's when you gaze out of the window and see nothing, because you're deep in thought.

I was ruminating about being unflappable. I wish I was unflappable – agents ought to be, but I'm not. Dad found a piece in a magazine about an unflappable butler the other day, and read it out to Mum and me.

It's a true story; it happened at a great house where they have a butler who stays calm whatever happens. One day a crippled Hurricane made a wheels-up landing in the grounds of the house, ploughed across their massive lawn at a rate of knots, crashed into the conservatory in a blizzard of splintered glass and came to a stop. The pilot clambered out unhurt, and the butler went to his master and said, 'There's a young man to see you, sir – he's in the conservatory.'

I loved it. Wished I was that butler.

'Price?' I jerked back to reality. Lines was looking at me. 'Are you all right, lad?'

'Y – yes, I was just thinking, sir.'

'You look a bit rocky – perhaps a breath of fresh air, eh? Splash of cold water?' He's all right, old Contour. Almost human.

I nodded. 'Yes, thank you, sir, I'll just . . .' I got out of my seat. I was tired, not ill at all, but a break is a break.

Lines turned to Linton. 'Go with him, Barker.'

We crossed the yard to the toilets. I dashed a handful of water onto my face, then nodded towards a cubicle. 'I'll sit down in there for a bit, if you don't mind hanging on?'

He grinned. ''Course I don't. Fag?' He held out the Woodbine packet.

'No thanks, but have one yourself. I won't be long.'

I pushed the door to, sat on the seat. I felt perfectly well, but I was in no rush to get back to Argentina and corned beef. I could hear Linton shuffling about outside, hawking and coughing. I thought some more about the unflappable butler, but doesn't time crawl when you want it to pass?

For something to do I started reading the graffiti that covered the door so densely you could hardly see the cream paint. It was vulgar stuff mostly, but some bits were quite funny.

I like grils was crossed out and corrected – **I like girls**. Under this in a different hand was, **What about us grils?**

I chuckled, then noticed a line in eye-catching green that read:

Sat same + same p same drill

I shook my head, but there was no mistaking the style. I'd been contacted again.

'All right now?' asked Linton when I emerged. I nodded. He dropped his tab-end, ground it under a heel. 'Good-o, it's nearly lunch time. Come on.'

I could have done with that Woodbine now, but it was too late.

FORTY-EIGHT
Linton Barker's Lungs

Saturday dawned and I was still unshot. This didn't make me unflappable, but I *had* simmered down a bit which was just as well, since it was time to carry out my third assignment.

In stories, agents never receive their instructions on lavatory doors. It felt disrespectful, and I wondered whether the chaps who don't mess around had chosen this way of showing their displeasure at my blabbing all over Farmer Giles. If so, I suppose I got off lightly.

It was a foggy morning, and I'm not talking

about mist. Everywhere was clotted with thick yellow stuff you could nearly gather by the armful and pile into a barrow. It was like cotton wool some giant had cleaned his filthy ears out with. I had to bike at about four miles a fortnight all the way to Myra Shay. It's a good job I'm familiar with the route, or I'd never have found the place at all.

When I did, the grass was cold and sodden. When I stretched out my arm my hand was invisible. If anybody else was barmy enough to be here, I didn't see 'em. In fact, Hitler could've landed three airborne divisions on Myra Shay that morning and nobody would've been any the wiser.

I groped my way to Manley's fence and peered through dripping mesh. I couldn't see the building, or even the cement path. If I sent the Skymaster over in this, the security man wouldn't see me do it, wouldn't know where to look.

What was I supposed to do? The chap couldn't know, when he scribbled on that lavatory door, that there'd be a peasouper on Saturday. Mind you, he couldn't know I'd be the one to read it, could he, out of a schoolful of kids? *Maybe he's a wizard*, I thought. *Knows everything*.

Which didn't help at all.

'That you, Biggles?' growled a nearby, sullen voice. I nearly jumped out of my skin. The watchman was a blob six feet away, on the other side of the fence. 'Y . . . yes,' I stammered, 'only it isn't Biggles, it's . . .'

'Whoa!' he bellowed like somebody stopping a runaway horse. 'Don't tell me your bleat'n name, you fathead. Fly the plane.'

I flew it. It vanished into the muck. The watchman vanished as well. I stuck my hands in my pockets and stood, screwing up my eyes into the fug. *Like standing in Linton Barker's lungs*, I thought.

It was a neat simile, but I hadn't long to enjoy it. As the blob reappeared, holding the plane aloft, somebody shouted and more blobs materialized, bobbing towards the watchman. He started to run, crying out as the phantom shapes merged with him. I heard a tearing, splintering noise, and knew that this time the Skymaster would fail to return.

I fled, thankful now for the fog.

FORTY-NINE
It Wasn't Exactly a Lie

I plunged through the noxious vapour, gibbering like an idiot. It took for ever to find the bike. The wet saddle soaked my pants, felt as though I needed my nappy changed. The only good thing was, whoever had pinched my plane wouldn't find me, let alone take pot shots.

I wobbled homeward. Or what I *hoped* was homeward. *Who were those fellows?* murmured a little voice in my head. *Germans? Traitors? Should I have stayed, helped the watchman? Sexton Blake would have. Yes, but* how, *with the fence between?*

Mum was washing spuds. She didn't peel 'em nowadays – it was a waste of good grub. There was a cartoon in the paper – a spud with arms and legs, wearing a jacket. *Good taste demands I keep my jacket on*, said the speech bubble. Old Hinkley reckons peeling spuds is as bad as signalling to enemy planes. *Mein Fuehrer, our agents in England are persuading housewives to peel potatoes: victory cannot be far away.*

I'd made up a story about the Skymaster. It wasn't exactly a lie. 'I lost the plane, Mum. It went over Manley's fence. I couldn't see because of the fog. Had to leave it.'

She sighed, shook her head. 'Never mind, love – perhaps they'll let you have it back if Dad telephones to them on Monday, explains it was an accident.'

'No!' I spoke more sharply than I'd meant to. Mum looked startled. 'I . . . don't think we should bother them, Mum. Kids lose planes at Manley's all the time, they're probably fed up to the back teeth with it.' Truth was, I doubted what me and the watchman had been up to at Manley's was strictly official. To alert the company might betray our secret.

Mum started grating a potato, she was making something called potato ring. 'Your brother gave you that aeroplane,' she murmured. 'It was his last gift to you. I'd have thought you'd want to have it back, if only as a keepsake.' Her voice wavered. 'Yes, that's it . . . a keepsake.' She dropped the grater and the potato and burst into tears. Feeling rotten for having snapped at her, I went to give her a hug like a Robinson probably would, and we were like that when Dad walked in.

FIFTY

Balls of Fragrant Smoke

'What's up – has something happened?' Dad nudged me aside, gripped Mum's shoulders. 'Tell me, Ethel.'

Mum shook her head. 'It's nothing, Frank. I'm being daft, that's all.' She pulled a hanky out of her pinny, dabbed her eyes. 'Gordon's lost the aeroplane Raymond gave him. It felt like another link broken – a link to him, I mean. Daft.' She blew her nose.

Dad looked at me. 'You didn't take the Skymaster out in this filthy fog, son, surely?'

I nodded dumbly.

'*Why*, for heaven's sake? You can't see your hand in front of your face out there. Didn't you realize the thing'd vanish as soon as you launched it?'

I nodded again. 'Yes, Dad, of course I did. But I *had* to go.'

He stared at me. 'Go – go *where*, Gordon? And why did you *have* to?'

I shook my head. 'I can't explain, Dad. It's . . . something I'm doing. For the war. It's a secret.'

'A secret.' He shook his head. 'Thirteen-year-old boys aren't *allowed* secrets, son. Not in this house, so you'd better tell me and your mother what you're up to, right now.' He led me through to the living room. Mum followed.

Well, I had to say *something*, didn't I? When you're thirteen, your parents are boss. I hadn't signed the Official Secrets Act.

'I'm doing it for Raymond,' I began. '*Was*, I mean. It's what he gave me the plane for.'

Mum made a mewing sound into her hanky.

Dad frowned at me. 'What on *earth* are you talking about, lad? Can't you see you're upsetting your mother?'

I nodded. 'I know, Dad, but it's true. I had to

buy the Skymaster and build it, then wait for instructions.'

'Instructions? From *who*, son?'

'I don't know. Some chaps who don't mess around, Raymond said.'

Mum was sobbing on the sofa. Dad looked dangerous.

'Look, son,' he growled, 'if you're making all this up, shooting some sort of line to glamourize yourself, you'd better stop this minute, because I'll not have your mother more distressed than she is already.'

I shook my head, pacing the room. 'You *asked* me, Dad. I'm not making anything up. Raymond was working for the Government.'

'*What?*'

'The Government. As an agent. He told me.' I looked at him. 'It's top secret. Raymond swore me to secrecy, so you've got to promise not to breathe a word to anyone. Mum too.'

Dad lowered himself into an armchair, motioned for me to take the other. He spoke quietly, with an expression on his face I couldn't read.

'Where did you fly the plane, son?'

'Myra Shay.'

'Myra Shay. How many times did you fly her there?'

'Three, including today.'

'And what happened when you flew her – the first two times, I mean?'

'Well, I had to send her over Manley's fence. As if it was by accident.'

'And then?'

'Well, then a fellow I call the watchman came and picked up the plane and wound up the engine and sent her back over.'

'Both times?'

'Yes.'

'Did this man – the watchman – do anything to the plane, besides wind the engine?'

'No.'

'And the plane itself – was there anything different about it when you got it back?'

'Not that I noticed.'

'Did you examine her at all – look inside perhaps?'

'No. My orders said not to.'

'And then you brought the plane straight home, put her in the shed?'

'Yes.'

'And then what?'

I shrugged. 'Then I waited for more orders. The last ones were on a lavatory door.'

'A lavatory door.' He'd been fiddling with his pipe. Now he put a match to it, puffed out balls of fragrant smoke. 'What happened today, son?'

I told him what had happened in the fog of Myra Shay. When I'd finished he sat silently smoking, gazing into the fire. Mum got up and went out to the kitchen. I sat staring at the carpet.

Mum brought tea. Dad said, 'Odd things happen in wartime, Gordon. We don't always get to know about them, but I'm pretty sure the Government isn't recruiting schoolboys as secret agents. Somebody recruited *you*, though, so perhaps I'm wrong.' He sipped his tea, then continued, 'Tell you what I want you to do. If any further orders arrive, even on lavatory doors, I want you to tell me before you carry them out.' I opened my mouth to protest, but he held up a hand. 'In return, I promise that your secret will be safe with your mother and me for as long as that remains possible. All right?'

Had to be all right, didn't it?

FIFTY-ONE
Two Policemen

I hadn't told my parents the most important bit – that Linton Barker saw someone he thought was Raymond, and I might have seen him myself. That would have set the cat among the pigeons and no mistake.

It was bad enough anyway. Mum kept giving me strange looks, and Dad hardly spoke to either of us. I wasn't sure they believed me, which was a rotten feeling. I felt awful about having spilled the beans so easily too. An agent who cracks when his dad questions him isn't likely to hold out long against the Gestapo.

One good thing though – my parents knew Raymond had been a hero. When that bomb got him, he was on his country's secret service. We could hold our heads up, like the parents of the late Michael Myers RN whose bike I now rode.

On Sunday morning I gave the bike a thorough clean and polish. It was a hero's bike, ridden by a hero's brother. When a little voice in my head whispered, *Yes, but what about* yourself? I drowned it out with whistling.

Monday morning was fogless, quite sunny for November. I was relieved nobody had come looking for the boy who'd fled Myra Shay on Saturday. The watchman couldn't split on me, of course – he didn't know me from Adam. And what we'd been doing, whatever it was, might be something and nothing anyway. Perhaps I'd hear no more about it.

I was kidding myself. Why would my brother have me build and fly that expensive model for something and nothing? And who'd take the trouble to contact me in a variety of novel ways for the sake of a prank? Dad's brooding silence ought to have told me he thought there was something serious behind it. But as I say, I was kidding myself.

It all began to unravel that day in the middle of double maths. There was a clatter of boots on parquet and the door banged open, but it wasn't Whitfield's dreaded storm troopers. It was old Hinkley, and he had two policemen with him.

FIFTY-TWO

The Dock

Oh yes, it was me they'd come for.

'The officers would like a word with you, Price,' said Hinkley. He led the way to his office and left me with them. I'd never cared for the old duffer, but I was sorry to see him go.

'Sit down, lad.' The senior officer nodded to the hard chair in front of the Head's desk. *The dock*, we called it. A pupil who found himself sitting on that chair was nearly always in trouble, and if he found himself lying across it with his bum in the air, the trouble was a bit more serious. The officer settled himself in Hinkley's leather swivel. His companion stood with his hands behind his back and his back to the window.

'I'm Detective Inspector Grant, and this is Detective Sergeant Dinsdale. And you are Gordon Price, is that right?'

I nodded. 'Yes, sir.'

'All right if we call you Gordon?'

'Yes.'

'Good. Well, Gordon, you know why we're here, don't you?'

'No, sir.'

'I think you *do*, lad. It's about your model aeroplane.'

'Which one?' I asked. 'I collect them.'

Grant shook his head. 'We're not concerned with your solids, Gordon. It's the Skymaster we're interested in. The flying model.'

'*Flying* model, sir?' I put on a puzzled face.

'That's what I said.'

'But I haven't *got* a flying model.' It wasn't a lie.

The detective sighed. 'We've checked with Carter's, lad. You bought a Skymaster from them last month – the only one they had in stock.'

'I lost it.'

He nodded. 'We *know* you lost it, Gordon,

because we found it, in a manner of speaking.'

'You *found* it?' I faked a happy smile. 'I'll get it back then, will I?'

'I don't think so, lad. It was carrying a cargo. A very valuable cargo. We suspect it had carried similar loads before.'

I didn't need to act flabbergasted – I was. 'Wh . . . what sort of cargo, sir?' I stammered.

Grant looked me in the eye. 'Don't you know?'

'No, sir, and if I *did* I couldn't tell you.'

'Why not, Gordon? *Why* couldn't you tell us?'

'Because it's a secret, sir. A state secret. I can't answer any more questions, I'm under orders.'

'Under orders?' Grant sighed again, leaned back in the chair and glanced across at his sergeant. 'I think we'd better have the parents in, Sergeant Dinsdale – down at the Station.' He looked at me. 'We'd like you to come with us, Gordon – we'll clear it with the headmaster. We need to ask you about these orders you've received, and it might be less . . . er . . . *unsettling* for you if your dad and mum are there.' He stood up. 'Shall we go?'

FIFTY-THREE
Not the Gestapo

It was my first time in a police car. Sergeant Dinsdale drove. Inspector Grant sat in the back with me. I was trying to be brave. *I won't tell you anything*, I thought. *Not even if you torture me.* Deep down though, I knew I would. I suppose I was pretty sure they wouldn't torture me anyway, especially with my parents there.

I was taken into a small room with no window. Mum and Dad were there, sitting on hard chairs in front of a wooden table. They looked awful. Mum had been crying. There was an empty chair.

'Sit down please, Gordon,' said the inspector. We were in a line: Mum then Dad then me. The two policemen sat behind the table.

Dad touched my sleeve. 'What's been going *on*, son?' he asked. 'This aeroplane business . . .'

'*We*'ll ask the questions, sir, if you wouldn't mind.' Dad sighed and sat back. Grant looked at me. 'Now, Gordon, there's nothing to be afraid of, we're not the Gestapo.'

'I know,' I said, 'and I'm not afraid.'

'Good.' He looked me in the eye. 'So – these orders you mentioned – who do they come from?'

'I don't know, sir.'

'You don't *know*?' He frowned. 'Then who told you to build the plane?'

I shook my head. 'I can't tell you, it's top secret.'

'Gordon.' Dad spoke sharply. 'It *isn't* top secret – it was Raymond.' He looked at Grant. 'His brother gave him money to buy the plane, Inspector.'

'*Dad!*' I gazed at him. 'You said it was safe with you, my secret. You *promised*. Now you're betraying Raymond. Betraying his *trust*.'

'Gordon?' The Inspector was looking at me.

'What secret did your brother trust to you?'

I looked at the floor. 'Do I *have* to answer, sir?'

He nodded. 'I'm afraid you *do*, laddie. Crimes have been committed. Serious in peacetime, more so because of the war. What did your brother tell you, exactly?'

'It . . . wasn't *crime*, sir, it was work for the Government. Raymond was an agent. He was helping the Government get an army together. A secret army, to fight the enemy after the ordinary army has been defeated and the Germans are here in England.'

Dad snorted. Grant looked at me.

'And do you think that'll happen, Gordon – an invasion, I mean?'

'I don't know, sir – it's what my brother told me. I suppose we have to be ready in case it does.'

Dad broke in. 'The boy's *plane*, Inspector – where does *that* fit in?'

Grant sighed. 'The Skymaster was used on three occasions to get industrial diamonds out of Manley's bonded premises, sir.' He gazed at Dad. 'You're an engineer, you don't need me to tell you how essential such diamonds are to the war effort.'

187

'And you're saying . . . you think my lad – *both* my lads – have been involved in *stealing industrial diamonds*?' Dad's tone was incredulous.

'I'm afraid so, sir,' said the inspector, 'though Gordon here obviously didn't know what was happening, having been told a story by his older brother.'

Mum burst into tears. Grant motioned to Sergeant Dinsdale, who helped her stand and steered her towards the door. Dad made to follow, but the inspector shook his head.

'There's more, Mr Price. It's probably best your wife hears it a bit later on, from you.'

Dad swallowed. '*More?* What can there be more? First we learn that our son is dead, then that he was a thief. What else is there, for pity's sake?'

Grant spoke softly. 'We have reason to believe your son is alive, sir.'

'*What?*' Dad stared. 'What're you *talking* about, man? Raymond's *dead*, they showed us his watch.'

'I *saw* him, Dad,' I burst out. 'Last week, biking home late from Norman's.' I *wanted* it to be true, wanted it so much I didn't think before I spoke.

Dad turned on me. 'You *saw* your brother and didn't tell your mother and me? When you *knew* how we were grieving?'

'I . . . I wasn't sure,' I stammered. 'It was dark. Linton Barker thought he saw him weeks ago as well, driving a car, but it could all have been a mistake, I didn't want to . . . you know . . . get Mum's hopes up.'

'*Hopes?*' Dad laughed harshly. 'If what we've heard here tonight is true, I'd rather he *was* dead.' He turned to Grant. 'Is that everything, Inspector, or do you have *more* revelations about my family? Perhaps my wife's been signalling to U-boats?'

I don't remember much after Mum and the U-boats. I was frightened, tired, confused. I thought Dad was being serious and it must've been too much for my brain, because it switched itself off.

FIFTY-FOUR
Rhinoceros

The inspector sent me to join Mum and a policewoman in another room. I was given a mug of tea. I don't suppose the Gestapo dishes out mugs of tea. Mum's eyes were red but she'd stopped crying. She said something to me, I don't know what, and I didn't reply. There was a stain on the lino shaped like a rhinoceros. I stared at it, warming my hands on the mug.

In the interview room, Dad was having to listen to stuff about Raymond that was even worse than what we'd heard. He broke it to Mum when Sergeant Dinsdale had driven us home. I'd gone straight to bed and out like a light, and neither of them ever told me. I picked it up bit by bit from things they said to each other: perhaps I was meant to.

Raymond never worked for the Government. He wasn't an agent, he was a spiv. In fact he was *worse* than a spiv. He was in a gang that stole scarce things, *rationed* things – petrol, tyres, cloth, industrial diamonds – and sold them on the black market. They pinched stuff like tea and sardines and silk stockings as well, and passed them to spivs who offered them on the street at outrageous prices. The gang carried guns, and at least one person had been shot by them.

And that wasn't the worst. The worst was, my brother and his friends – the chaps who *don't mess around* – robbed the dead. In the blackout they'd hurry to places where people had been killed by bombs, and steal their identity cards and ration books. They took rings and watches and cash too, but what they wanted most was the cards and ration books, because with those they could swap identities, leaving their own cards on the bodies so the police would think *they'*d been killed. Inspector Grant told Dad he thought

Raymond had swapped identities with a man called Stanton Lander, which is why the Army had stopped looking for him. We'd buried Lander with my brother's watch on his wrist and my brother's papers in his wallet. Raymond was alive and at large, only everybody thought his name was Stanton Lander.

I know it's a horrible thing to say, but I wasn't glad my brother was alive. He'd told me wicked lies and made a criminal of me, pretending he was making me a hero. Pretending he was a hero.

So no, I wasn't glad, and I wondered if that meant I was as bad as him.

FIFTY-FIVE
Kitten

They didn't send me to school next day, but I crept there on Wednesday in a blue funk, recalling Whitfield's terrible indictment of the spiv. *Parasite . . . black marketeer . . . stealing goods that belong to the whole nation . . . helping the enemy . . . a traitor . . . . the lowest of the low . . . sell his mother if he could get half a crown for her . . .*

I didn't take the bike. It had been a hero's bike – I wasn't fit to clean it, let alone ride it.

As it turned out, nothing much happened at school. Linton Barker asked what the police had wanted, and I lied. Well, lying's nothing compared to the stuff I'd done already. I told him they'd found my model plane and I had to identify it. Daft story, but Linton believed it – goes to show nicotine rots the brain.

I don't know how much Hinkley knew, but he didn't expel me or even send for me. None of the teachers said anything either. That was a relief, I can tell you. Not that this was the end of it – I knew there'd be the devil to pay when the police caught up with Raymond, which sooner or later they would. It'd be in the papers then, and I'd have to kill myself.

If school wasn't so bad, home was horrible. Dad just about managed to drag himself off to work every morning, but Mum moped and wept and finally took to her bed. Gran had to move across from Hastley to look after us all.

I was scared stiff all the time, wondering how many years I'd get for stealing three lots of diamonds, and what prison would be like. I could hardly sleep at night for worrying about it. When I mentioned it to Gran she said, 'They won't send you to prison, sweetheart, you're too young. And anyway they know you didn't mean to steal – you were tricked into it by that useless brother of yours.'

It's funny, but even now I didn't like to hear Raymond slandered. I hated him, but every evening when Dad put up my brother's blackout boards, I found myself wondering where he was, what he was doing. I hoped he wasn't shooting anybody, because they'd hang him if he was.

I was missing Norman, but shame prevented my calling on the Robinsons. I'd have to avoid mentioning the nightmare my brother's activities had plunged us into. Either that or tell them everything. I knew they'd be sympathetic if I did, but my parents would be mortified: those particular beans weren't really mine to spill.

November gave way to December. There hadn't been a raid for weeks, but a few nights before Christmas there was a heavy one. It was a Thursday. Mum refused to get up to go to the shelter, so neither Dad nor Gran would go either. They made *me* go, so it was just me and the Andersons. It was a long night.

No bombs fell anywhere near us, but something awful happened just the same. First assembly after the hols, Hinkley stood on the platform and told us about a pupil called Betty Farfield.

The Farfields lived a few streets away from us. The night of the raid, Betty had gone with her mum, dad, sister and kitten to their shelter. At the height of the raid, the kitten panicked and leaped out. Before her parents knew what was happening, the girl went after it. She was crossing their lawn when a piece of shrapnel from our ack-ack struck her on the head. Her dad ran to her but she was dead.

FIFTY-SIX
Shrapnel

And that's the thing about war. Betty Farfield died, but the Germans didn't kill her. Thousands were killed in training accidents, and civilians died of hunger and disease far away from any fighting. And then there were those like Betty's parents and my mum, who didn't actually die, but something inside them did, so that they were never the same afterwards. War is a sort of invisible shrapnel that rips through people's lives. It hit me, but I was lucky – it didn't find a vital spot and my wound healed, though not straight away.

Not straight away. On Christmas Eve I wheeled Michael Myers's bike all the way to Hastley like a sad Santa, and left it propped against his parents' house with a note taped to the saddle:

This is a hero's bike: spivs keep off.

Talk about cheesed off. The real Santa brought me a wizard kit to build a Dornier 17, but it failed to lift my spirits. And no – I *don't* believe in him. How would he cope with barrage balloons? With shrapnel?

FIFTY-SEVEN
Auld Lang Syne

My brother came home on New Year's Eve, but nobody sang 'Auld Lang Syne'. It was ten o'clock, and a filthy night. The wind roared round the house, flinging ice flack at the windows. We didn't plan to see the new year in, but Mum was downstairs for the first time in weeks, which is why I was still up.

We had the radio on, Sandy McPherson at the organ. There was a crash, the side door flying open, we thought by itself. A gust slammed into the room. Dad rose with an oath, half out of the armchair when Raymond burst in.

We didn't know him. A wind-battered figure in a sodden mac, unshaven, hair plastered to his skull. Torn trousers, broken shoes, no socks. *Escaped POW* our first thought. Until he spoke.

'Help me, Dad, Mum,' he croaked. 'They'll be here in a minute, you haven't seen me.' He whirled, stumbled to the stairs and up. None of us had spoken, there hadn't been time. We were in the hallway, gawping up, when the police came swarming through the kitchen. There were only seconds between Raymond's arrival and theirs – he could be heard on the landing when they barged past us. I don't know if we'd have hidden him, because we didn't get the chance. One minute he was that desperate stranger in the doorway, the next he was being bundled down the stairs and out the house by a knot of panting constables.

Sergeant Dinsdale stayed to do the commentary. 'Sorry about that,' he gasped, looking ruffled. 'Must've shocked you all a bit, but there wasn't time to ... you know ... knock.'

'My boy,' cried Mum. 'Where's he being taken to? What'll happen to him, Sergeant?' Her voice broke. 'You won't let them *hurt* him, will you?'

Dad put his arms round her, shushed her, stroked her hair.

The sergeant shook his head. 'Nobody'll hurt your son, Mrs Price. He'll be detained at police headquarters overnight and interviewed tomorrow.' He shrugged. 'After that I don't know – depends how co-operative he is, I suppose.'

He left without wishing us a happy new year. It'd have sounded a bit hollow, I expect, after what had just happened.

FIFTY-EIGHT
Heinkel

It sent Mum a bit doolally, which is a shame because she'd been showing signs of recovery. It was ten-past ten, but instead of going to bed she went up to Raymond's room and started pulling clothes out of his drawers, arranging them in neat piles on the bed. It was eleven before Dad and Gran persuaded her to stop.

Next morning, New Year's Day, she brought the things downstairs in a suitcase. 'Take this to the police station, Frank,' she told Dad, 'and give it to Raymond.'

'Ethel, love,' he protested, 'You can't just walk

into police HQ and demand to see someone they're holding.'

Mum glared at him. 'Did you see the state of him last night – those wet rags he was wearing? He can't live in those for the rest of his life. Ask to see him, and if they won't let you, leave the suitcase with them. Inspector Grant's a nice enough fellow – he'll see Raymond gets it.'

Dad didn't want to go. As he'd said, he'd rather see my brother dead than a criminal. But he loved Mum, and he could see this really mattered to her.

'I'll come with you if you like, Frank,' offered Gran, but he shook his head.

'I'd sooner you stayed with Ethel, Mum. Gordon'll keep me company, won't you, son?'

And that's how I found myself walking with Dad through deserted Bank-Holiday streets at eight o'clock on a raw, damp morning. If there'd been anyone about, they'd have thought we were doing a flit. A flit's when you owe rent and can't pay, so you pack up and leave while your landlord's asleep in his bed. Or they might think we'd murdered someone and cut her up and put the bits in the suitcase, like Buck Ruxton a few years ago.

I hoped they wouldn't let us see Raymond. I wouldn't know what to say to him. I mean, I'd be lying if I told him I hoped they wouldn't send him to prison. I didn't hope that. I hoped they *would* send him, he deserved it. But I couldn't tell him that, could I? *Hello, Raymond, I hope you get ten years.* You can't say that to your brother, even if he *is* the king of the spivs. No, I hoped we'd drop his togs off and leave.

We were twenty yards from police HQ when I saw the Heinkel.

FIFTY-NINE
What Was Left of it

It was coming in low, trailing black smoke from one engine. In the seconds before it hit, I thought I glimpsed the pilot through the perspex nose, fighting for control. If so, he fought in vain. The machine maintained its shallow dive till it struck the double doors of the police station and blew up.

The whole unbelievable event can't have occupied more than a few seconds, but it seemed to take place in slow motion. When the crash became inevitable I hit the pavement in a graceless dive, knocking the breath from my lungs. I sensed Dad flinging himself flat just beyond my sight. The blast followed at once, slamming into my face like a hot muffler. A screechy din tore through my eardrums into my skull. Heavy lumps pattered down, making the ground jump. I flattened my face on the flags and screwed up my eyes, waiting for some falling thing to squash me.

It didn't happen. The din subsided, replaced by a crackling noise and acrid fumes that stung my nose and throat. I opened streaming eyes and saw the building on fire.

'Raymond!' Dad plunged past, choking out my brother's name. Only then did it reach my brain that Raymond was somewhere inside, trapped by locks and bars. I got up and tottered after my father.

We didn't find him – it was impossible. The place, what was left of it, was black with smoke. Our eyes burned, we could hardly breathe let alone call his name. We knew there was a basement with cells where he'd be, but we couldn't find the stairs. Didn't recognize anything, everything was smashed. After what felt like hours, Dad found somebody alive behind a drunken counter and signalled me to help. The fellow was in a bad way – his scalp was bloody and his head lolled when Dad got his hands under his armpits and lifted. I took the legs. The fire was taking hold, spreading. Terrific heat, suffocating fumes. We staggered past a buckled propeller, a blackened engine, the stump of a wing. The doors were a great ragged hole where light was, and air. I'll never know how we reached it. All I know was that we were standing on the pavement, looking down at the constable we'd dragged out, when firemen and wardens arrived and made us lie on stretchers.

Nothing was hurting, but I think I fell asleep.

SIXTY
Chop Some Bits Off

'Oh, so you do spend some time awake, old chap – I'd begun to think I was wasting my time.'

'Huh?' I rolled my head on the pillow. Norman was gazing at me from a chair by the bed.

'Hello, Norman, what're *you* doing here?'

He pulled a face. 'Visiting *you*, you chump, what else?'

'But how did you know I was here?'

He arched his brow. '*Everybody* knows, old man, you're quite famous, y'know.'

'F . . . famous? *Me?*'

'Yes, *you*.' He frowned. 'Oh, I say, you haven't lost your *memory* have you? You do *remember* snatching Constable Whitfield from the jaws of death?'

'Constable . . . ? Oh yeah, but Dad did it.' Sudden fear stabbed me. 'Where *is* my dad, is he all right?'

Norman nodded. 'He's fine, old chap. Absolutely top hole. Men's surgical, down the corridor.' He looked solemn. 'They . . . didn't reach your brother in time though, old chap. I'm most awfully sorry.'

I shook my head. 'Thanks, I never expected they would.'

A nurse appeared. 'I hope this young man isn't bothering you, Gordon?' she smiled.

'Oh, he *is*, nurse,' I told her. 'He kicked me, then emptied a bedpan on my head. I think you should operate, chop some bits off.'

She nodded. 'I'll mention it to Matron.'

When the nurse had gone, Norman filled me in on a few things. He told me Dad and I had been here two days, suffering from smoke inhalation. They'd send us home soon. The constable was here too, but in the burns unit. He'd be staying for a while. Mum was bad with her nerves: she wasn't up to visiting. Gran came to see me yesterday, but I was asleep. And we were in the local paper, Dad and me:

Father and Son in Daring Rescue.

He'd save his parents' copy for me.

He's a super chap, old Norman – best chum a fellow could wish for. He'd even brought *grapes*, for goodness' sake. When I asked how he'd managed *that* in wartime, he grinned and said, 'Sarah found 'em somewhere.'

SIXTY-ONE
A Gong

We went home next day, Dad and me. Mum was limp as a rag but Gran was her old brisk self, conjuring tasty meals out of very little. Coping.

The doctor kept me off school for a week or two. I was glad. I didn't know what sort of reception to expect there – as the brother of a heartless spiv, or the gallant rescuer of PC Whitfield.

That was the worst bit, by the way. Unless you're pretty dim, you'll have spotted that the constable had the same surname as my maths

211

teacher. And you're right, they were father and son. I'd no idea how Whitfield would react to having his son's rescuer sitting in front of him every Monday morning. Would he feel obliged to go easy on me, make me ink monitor or something?

I found out when I went back, and the answer was a resounding no. I suppose he was anxious not to be seen to favour me so he did the opposite, picking on me for the sake of it, whacking me with the famous cane for things like breathing, or having one eye slightly larger than the other.

We'd been home a few days when Detective Inspector Grant knocked on the front door. I thought he'd come to arrest me, but he hadn't. He'd come on behalf of the force, to thank Dad and me officially for our rescue of one of his men.

'Oh, and it's been decided that no further action will be taken in the matter of you and your model aeroplane, Gordon,' he added. I wasn't half relieved.

He told Dad something else while Mum, Gran and I were in the kitchen, brewing tea and searching for a biscuit to offer him. He said if it was any consolation, Raymond would probably have been hanged: a man had been shot dead, and although my brother hadn't actually fired the gun, he'd been with the man who had. Dad told us later, and I suppose it *did* console us in a way. Better the Heinkel than sitting in a condemned cell, ticking off those last, ghastly hours.

Months later, after I'd turned fourteen, said goodbye to Foundry Street School and gone to work with Dad at Beresford's, we learned that Dad was to get a George Medal, while I would be presented with an illuminated testimonial on parchment. I wasn't at all sure we deserved these honours. Well, we didn't go into that burning building to rescue Constable Whitfield – we went to get Raymond out. The rescue was really a sort of accident. It wasn't till years later that I realized lots of gallant acts are probably accidental in one way or another – rushes of blood to the head, perhaps. In my view, something Dicky Deadman did one day in our final term was far braver than my effort.

We were doing English with Thrasher Waxman, who was mad keen on poetry. He'd written these lines on the blackboard:

What was he doing, the great god Pan,
Down in the reeds by the river?

when he was summoned to go see old Hinkley.
While he was out of the room, Dicky went up to
the board and scrawled,

having a pee probably

underneath. Crude and silly, yes, but suicidally
brave against a teacher who wasn't called
Thrasher for nothing. Deadman was never a
chum of mine, but he earned a gong that day.

Funny thing though, heroism. If you believe
the papers, our enemies are never heroes,
they're mad fanatics. Why should all the heroes
be on our side?

SIXTY-TWO

What Happened Afterwards

Anything else? Oh yes – what happened afterwards.

Well, my brother had dodged justice in a way, but others didn't. To my amazement, Contour Lines was among those arrested, along with the caretaker. They'd played supporting roles in Raymond's sleazy drama – most of my so-called orders had come through them. The young assistant at Carters was in it as well, and all three went to prison.

I got off scot-free, but I think it's only fair to admit that I hadn't been totally innocent myself in the matter of the black market. I'd been willing enough to eat my share of Sarah's goodies, and without people like me the spivs would have had no customers.

I turned seventeen and a half (old enough to join up) one month after Japan surrendered. I'd missed the war, but I enlisted in the RAF anyway. They turned me down for pilot training – my trig wasn't good enough – so I mustered as an air gunner. I did five years, mostly boring patrols over the Baltic. Then I went back to Beresford's to work with Dad.

My best chum Norman joined the RAF too, but not until he'd qualified as a doctor. He enlisted just as I completed my five, and we kept in touch by post while he served at Nocton Hall RAF hospital near Nottingham, and at Wegberg in Germany. He's a GP now, like his father, who discovered in 1948 how we'd vandalized his aluminium car, and didn't care: he was far too busy helping to operate the brand new National Health Service.

Dicky Deadman did nine years in the Navy, then set up as an estate agent. I bought my house from him and it was fine, so he never did become a spiv.

The last I heard of Walter Linfoot, he was a long-distance lorry driver.

Poor Linton Barker died at 36 from lung cancer, to nobody's surprise.

Herbert and Florrie Anderson retired to Skegness.

P.C. Whitfield recovered from his burns – he's a Chief Inspector in the Met.

Oh, I nearly forgot the best bit. When Dad and I got home from hospital that day in 1941, Michael Myers's bike was leaning on the shed. My note was still taped to the saddle, but somebody had scribbled out the second part so that it read:

This is a hero's bike.